The Fallen

By
Roy Love

PublishAmerica
Baltimore

Hardcover 978-1-4512-2309-5
Softcover 978-1-4512-2310-1
PUBLISHED BY PUBLISHAMERICA, LLLP
www.publishamerica.com
Baltimore

Printed in the United States of America

Acknowledgements:

Support for the book came most in part from my family and my wife, Emma. Without their support, this book would never have been a reality. Also, with the main character being named after our son, I'm sure his first bedtime story will be interesting! While all characters in this novel are fictional, there are several individuals who have lent their personalities to make the characters unique.

To Tom Savini

Enjoy the Book

Ray K

Characters:

What many people do not know is that the characters in the book are modeled after some of the people who I have the pleasure of knowing. The villain in this story is modeled after my best friend, whom I have known for nearly twenty years, and while not a villain in real life, the rivalry that we have shared since kindergarten is what inspired the character. Ironically, several of the characters in this book are based off of people that I speak to on a daily basis, but whom I have never met face to face. A special thank you goes out to my friends who have lent me their personalities and their voices which inspired these characters. Because I don't want to put real names in here, thank you to Enkidu, Suspect, and Shadowwolf (you know who you are) for the rather intriguing conversations and the laughs we have shared.

Prologue
Genesis

Exiting the plane of his private Leer jet, Martin Bishop and his assistant Clayton Lang moved toward the black stretch limousine waiting near the side of the private runway. They had come to Shanghai, China to make and exchange that would save Martin Bishop from certain poverty. Although he still owned the Leer jet, his career had come to an abrupt halt with the liquidation of his company. The production of micro processors had taken a turn for the worse with the integration of the newest company, "Techmill". The new production line of Techmill had revolutionized the industry, able to produce the chips at incredible speed and without having to pay workers to man the machines. *Putting me out of business has been their plan all along,* Martin Bishop thought. Once the new giant had been able to produce the microprocessors three times faster than Bishop's company, a buyout was inevitable.

This will put me back on the map, Bishop thought as he and his assistant stepped into the limo. Excited and nervous at the same time, Bishop anticipated no problems with the exchange. Of course, trading twenty guidance chips used in nuclear missiles to a rogue Chinese general would be construed as treason to the United States, but how could anyone possibly know that the exchange took place or who sold them to the Chinese. Bishop acquired these chips at the high cost of everything he owned. China was paying dearly for the trade however, quadruple what Bishop paid.

The Limousine pulled off the runway and through a private gate on the west end of the small airport. Staying quiet for more than half of the trip, the two men just stared out of the window nervous about what was to transpire. It was Clayton that broke the still silence of the soundproof back seat.

"What the hell are we doing Martin"

"Having Second thoughts," asked Bishop.

"Hell yes I'm having second thoughts, we could be signing the death warrant for millions of people by selling these chips, not to mention ours it the U.S. Government gets wind of this, and they know everything Martin."

moved the weapon in the direction of Martin and fired two shots which landed into the oak door. Bishop rushed for the door again hearing the distinct "TINK" of David Tanaka's weapon. Martin Bishop knew that he had been hit as a tremendous pressure in his lower back pushed him forward. Bishop managed to find the strength to lunge for the door once again. This time, before Bishop could think, the door exploded inward with a flash of bright white light and a deafening explosion. Martin Bishop was stunned by the flash grenade that had blown the door from its hinges. Pouring into the room was a mix of Chinese Military and CIA field agents all with weapons raised. The point man for the Military shouted something in Chinese toward David Tanaka, which Bishop figured to be "Drop your weapon." Another soft "TINK" of Davids weapon and the point man fell face down onto the floor not moving. One of the agents from the CIA turned his weapon to David and fired, double tapping him in the chest. The General's son fell back into his chair where he sat motionless.

Bishop paid no attention to General Tanaka as his hands raised in surrender. His only concern was checking on the lifeless form of Clay lying on the floor. As Bishop fell to his knees and checked Clay's carotid artery for a pulse, and found nothing. A medic with the CIA had dropped his bag near Bishop, and also checked for a pulse on Clay. The medic, looking distraught then turned to Bishop and started checking his wound.

"Not me," shouted Bishop. "Clay needs help!"

The medic continued to look at Bishop's wound with no interest in Clay. Bishop again shouted at the medic but to no avail. He knew then, that his assistant was dead.

Bishop lay on a gurney outside of the restaurant being treated by the same CIA medic and several members of the Ambulance crew. They were stringing lines of saline and morphine above his head and inserting multiple large bore IV's into his forearm. Looking back toward the restaurant, he saw the Chinese Military leading General Tanaka out of the entryway and toward a large armored car. The General looked up spotting Bishop and suddenly broke away from his captors moving with lightning speed toward Bishop.

"You took my son from me Bishop, MY SON! Expect your just deserts soon," shouted Tanaka.

The Military finally wrestled Tanaka down to the ground and got him under control. Bishop watched as they lead Tanaka into the armored truck and drove away.

CIA Field Agent Baker, Bishop's contact with the Agency approached with longing in his eyes.

"Sorry about your friend Martin. I wish we could have entered a few seconds sooner."

"Me too," muttered Bishop. What will happen to him now?"

Baker looked almost sorry for Tanaka as he peered down the long street where the truck had sped off.

"The Chinese have a special place for people like him... Poor bastard," he said.

Bishop finally realized the implications of what Tanaka had said to him. Thinking back, *expect your just deserts soon* he had said. Bishop's eyes widened.

"My daughter Baker, he is going to kill my daughter!"

Chapter 1
The Angel of Death

Gabriel Mason walked into the dimly lit briefing room of Choir Headquarters. Located in New York City, this thirty story building was home to the world's top assassins. This of course, was not what the entire building was dedicated to. For security reasons it was wise to have a dummy corporation set up on the lower floors to throw off any would-be do-gooders. The first ten floors of this office building acted as an insurance brokerage. *It was convenient having the insurance agency on the floors below,* Gabriel thought. They kept files on some of the most wealthy business men in the United States, letting him do his job much smoother.

Sitting at the large cherry conference table in the middle of the room, Gabriel leaned back and placed his feet on the table, something he knew his handler Marcus truly hated. Looking around the room, some of the top agents of the Choir were also present, which was fairly unusual. Typically a briefing is done with each agent individually due to secrecy. Today, Gabriel was not the only first class ranked assassin in the room. To his left sat Raphael, the tallest and one of the strongest of the Choir's assassins. Next sat Uriel; a devilish looking African American and a master of explosives. They call in Uriel when they want someone burned beyond recognition. The other two first class members were Ariel, and Jeremiel. Everyone had a specific way of killing someone, and the members in this room were considered some of the best.

Gabriel thought back to working with Ariel in 2006. They sat in a small pub in Northern Ireland, their target Collin McNichol was on the other end of the bar. They were assigned to McNichol due to his killing of so many innocents while in the IRA. Collateral damage was one thing, but blowing up busses full of civilians had gotten him to the top of the list. Ariel picked him up in the bar, took him back to her hotel room, then proceeded to maim and kill him. She was definitely someone Gabriel never wanted to cross.

For the past ten months Gabriel was training Jeremiel with his partner Alexander to operate point, which meant he set up and made the kill. Jeremiel preferred to do everything quietly. Gabriel was truly amazed at how silent and gentle Jeremiel was with his targets; it was as if they never felt the deathblow. That, Gabriel thought, made Jeremiel one of the most potent killers in the Choir. Jeremiel had just been promoted to first class last month and had already taken out two high priority targets as he ws quickly rising to the top.

Gabriel, now back on point was the only assassin to work with a partner. Many assassins thought it was better to work alone, but Gabriel knew that in order to stalk your target successfully, you need constant surveillance. At the age of twenty three years old, Gabriel had risen quickly through the ranks displaying an obvious talent for the business. There was only one person stronger, smarter, and faster than Gabriel and that was Michael. Being recruited by Michael was a good thing for Gabriel, *it was better than death after all*, Gabriel thought.

After nearly thirty minutes Marcus walked into the room, closing the door silently behind him. Taking his seat at the head of the oval table, Marcus pulled multiple files out of his briefcase. Briefly looking at each file, he slid them to their respective agents. Sitting high in his chair, he began muttering something to Uriel about his assignment. Gabriel had always pretended to tune out the assignments of others but really heard every word of the briefing.

Marcus then turned to Raphael and noticed Gabriel's feet on the table.

"Comfortable Gabriel, or would you like a pillow?"

"Nah, I'm good," chuckled Gabriel.

Gabriel took that as his cue to remove his feet. No one had ever been killed for that, but Marcus might give him several boring jobs for it.

"Raphael, your target is Gene Hershey, age fifty five, Manhattan New York. He is a Catholic Priest who has been making headlines for his interest in young altar boys. Our contractor would like it messy, so try to make it look like an angry parent took matters into their own hands."

Raphael just nodded, with a smile on his face, meaning he was pleased to be working so close to HQ.

"Gabriel, your job is a little more unusual than normal."

"Great," said Gabriel obviously frustrated.

"Your target is Cady Bishop, a nineteen year old female from Shaver Lake, California. Our contractor would also like some suffering to be involved. Due to the small population of the town however, we have opted for a quick and quiet operation to minimize your exposure. Due to the nature of this operation, our contractor feels that the girl may know more than she lets on. They would like primary surveillance of the target as well as known contacts. See what she knows before you take her out."

"What in the world could a nineteen year old girl have done to draw our attention," Gabriel asked.

"Unknown at this time, but we will fill you in as we receive more information. Gabriel, this mission is priority one."

Gabriel knew what Marcus was implying by saying priority one. It meant that someone had contracted the Choir to kill the girl, offering well over a million dollars.

"So basically, we are getting paid an obscene amount of money."

"Basically," said Marcus.

Gabriel sat and examined the file while the briefing continued. He found his usual fake ID, passport, equipment list, plane tickets, etc. *Something is definitely odd about this job,* he thought. Looking up at Marcus, he could see the tall blond man speaking to Jeremiel. Marcus, who stood almost 6'7", and weighed 200 pounds, was not the man you wanted to mess with in this agency. He took care of the day to day operations of the assassins, and as Gabriel knew, was the leader of the Choir; something that he didn't like to boast about. It was his idea to name everyone after Angels, and the Choir fell right in line with it. Now every assassin in the building was named after one Angel or another. The individuals sitting at this table were the most highly ranked of the Choir's assassins. Named after the Arc-Angels, they embodied the best the Choir had to offer. Other members of the Choir only aspire to get to this level, but many fail.

When the briefing had concluded, Gabriel stayed seated as everyone left the room. Marcus sat motionless, staring at Gabriel.

"Problem Gabriel?"

"You could say that. What's with sending me across the country to kill a nineteen year old girl?" This could be done by a Class four member."

"Gabriel, I know your one of the best, and that is what was requested. I promised to put my top man on this file, and you're it."

"Your top man is Michael," Gabriel retorted.

"Michael is otherwise engaged in Turkey. I need a first class agent on this, and if you're refusing, I can always try to find another boring errand for you to run.

"No, I'll take the job, but when I get back, I want something important."

"Setting terms Gabriel?"

"You know it."

"I'll check into it while you are out on this job, I will try to find something more suited to your skill level.

"And pay grade," Gabriel butted in.

"And pay grade," Marcus said with his usual smile.

Chapter 2
Identity Crisis

Cady Bishop walked through the Forrest Hills mall with her best friend Jan Siduri. The expansive mall was home to over two hundred stores. Most of the stores Cady didn't care for but Jan was a shop-a-holic and that meant going into every one of them. Cady liked coming to the mall, it was her chance to escape from the confines of her house and overprotective father. Lately, he had been more and more anal about where she could go, what she could do and who she could talk to. She suspected it had something to do with his latest trip to China, but it didn't matter, she insisted that he stop treating her like a child and let her go out with her friends. Jan was the perfect escape from the over protectiveness of her father so she did not mind spending the entire day at the mall with her, even if it meant watching her spend all of her money on things she didn't need.

After a few clothing stores, Jan could tell that Cady was hungry so it was off to the food court. Cady and Jan had split up to get their favorite foods and met at the same table. Cady could never pass up the Japanese food, and Jan had gotten chicken fingers from McDonalds. Cady was halfway through her shrimp tempura when a loud crash and a lot of yelling erupted behind her. She turned to see a girl throwing her tray at her boyfriend and screaming at the top of her lungs.

"Boys," Jan said in a huff.

"What happened back there? Why are they fighting like that?"

Jan looked at Cady with a sly smile, "He was checking you out and his girlfriend caught him".

"Oh God," Cady sighed putting her head in her palms.

Cady was no stranger to men looking at her; standing 5"10 and weighing 120 pounds, with straight brown hair to her shoulder blades and bright green eyes. Cady hated when boys stared at her, she suspected them all of looking at her chest anyway. Since her freshman year of high school she had not dated anyone for that reason. Nobody was ever interested in what she had to say, just getting her into bed.

Cady and Jan both stood up and walked out of the food court toward the elevator leading to the second floor. Still thinking of what happened in the food court; Cady did not notice that Jan was no longer walking beside her. Instead she was speaking to a boy that had approached her. Turning around to walk back to Jan, she was awestruck at how similar Jan and the boy looked. Jan stood 5'10" also, Cady guessed around 130 pounds, with long blond hair and blue eyes. The boy was exactly the same height with dirty blond hair that was made to look messed. Walking closer she could see that the boy had blue eyes also.

By the time Cady had reached Jan, she was already writing her phone number on the boys' hand. Jan was like that, she was the exact opposite of Cady, always finding new and exciting boyfriends. Finally reaching the two, Jan had turned from the boy to Cady and motioned for her with her eyes darting back to the boy.

"Cady Bishop, this is Alex Brody," she said trying to hide her excitement.

Cady now saw that the boy was even better looking up close. Although, Cady thought, he and Jan could be brother and sister.

"Hi," Cady said with a smile and reaching out to shake his hand. Alex reached out and did the same. Alex moved uncomfortably close to Cady and whispered in her ear.

"Your friend seems to like me, what do you think?"

Cady decided to have fun with this one, and whispered back, "She likes anything with two legs and a heartbeat."

"Cold, really cold," he said as he pulled away from her.

"Well girls, I have to get going and pick up my brother before he gets too impatient, I'll give you a call Jan."

"You had better," Jan said in an excited tone.

Walking away seemed hard for Jan, as if she wanted to stay there and talk for hours. Walking toward the elevator, Jan was now looking intently at her cell phone as if expecting a call or text message from Alex so quickly. Looking disappointed she put the phone back in her jacket just as they entered the elevator.

Finally entering the store that Cady actually wanted to shop in was refreshing. She looked around for a new jacket that she had seen previously. Finally finding it near the back of the store, she picked it up and headed for the counter. Jan, as far as she could tell was no longer shopping, she just kept checking her cell phone waiting for Alex to call. When she reached the counter a nicely dressed woman dropped what she as doing to check her out.

"Find everything ok," asked the woman.

"Yep, I've wanted this jacket for weeks."

"Good thing you came in today, that's the last one."

Reaching into her purse to find her wallet, she came up empty. Looking into the bag, she could find no trace of her wallet or her cell phone. Distressed, she quickly walked away from the counter toward Jan.

"What's up, where's your jacket?"

"Alex, Alex, did you get his phone number?"

"No why," said Jan startled.

"He stole my wallet and cell phone!"

Looking over the rail of the third floor of the mall, Gabriel stood motionless, watching his target fret over her lost items. Sensing that Alex was close behind him, he stayed still, watching the confusion.

"Did you get everything," asked Gabriel.

"Yea," said Alex as he handed Gabriel the items.

They moved away from the railing and searched through the wallet. The contents included a driver's license, two credit cards, and a gym membership. Now examining the cell phone, Gabriel flipped through all of the contacts memorizing the ones with a photo on the caller ID, knowing those would be her closest friends. Looking back at the driver's license Gabriel found the spelling of her name interesting. Cady, was pronounced Katie. *Why do parents do this to their children*, thought Gabriel.

"Great start, do we have enough to move on this?"

"Not yet, but soon," said Gabriel.

Chapter 3
Plan of Attack

Getting to know your target personally is never a good idea. Gabriel rarely ever let his mark see him let alone stand there and shake hands with him. Several problems can arise from getting up close and personal with your target. First, they could always blow your cover, and if that were to happen, game over, either kill them right then and there or miss your chance forever. Another reason is the risk of being seen by friends, family, etc. If something like that were to happen, there is a high probability of a manhunt and the arrest of said assassin. Not that the police pose much of a threat to a trained killer, but it's what happens to you while you are incarcerated. Chances are, you would not last the night if the Choir found out about your capture. They don't like loose ends, and neither does Gabriel. Several times he had to access a high security prison to *dispose* of compromised agents.

With all of this running through his head, he couldn't help but worry about their surveillance post. Moving into a third floor apartment where they could survey the marks house from across the street was a giant risk, one he was almost not willing to take. The only reason he was taking this risk is due to the new information he received from the Choir via a secure connection on his laptop. The girl was now on the open market for any assassin to take the bounty on her head. What had she had done to deserve the attention of every assassin in the world? Either way, he had to make his move in the next few days or all hell would be raining down on the target. Other assassins are sloppy. They will plant some C4 and blow up your house then sort through the rubble dressed as a firefighter to find confirmation of the kill. This was not Gabriel's style. He liked everything quick and clean. Thinking to himself that he originally wanted to make it look like she had died in her sleep or from a drug overdose was out. There were too many motion detectors to sneak into the house without getting personal with her. He had decided on a sniper rifle that he had picked up in Switzerland on one of his last kills. A Sig 550 Sniper complete with silencer and sub-sonic ammo. This way, if he takes the shot from his window in the apartment, no one would be able to hear it. By the time the local police arrived and traced the trajectory beck to Gabriel's position, he and Alex would be back at headquarters being debriefed.

Being that Gabriel and his partner had moved in across the street, it was easy to survey the target from the living room window. Across the street, the house was more mansion like than Gabriel was used to. Although the easiest part of the job would be taking the kill shot. He had a complete view of the marks bedroom. Gabriel thought about being humane and waiting until the girl fell asleep but he decided there was too much risk of the bullet ricocheting off the glass of the window, he would have to have her standing to take the shot.

Beginning surveillance was Alex's job. He sat at the window with a range finder and laptop. Meanwhile, Gabriel downloaded the contact list from the marks phone and cloned it to his back up cell phone so that anyone who called her he would also be able to hear. Gabriel loved technology, cell phones made it so easy to track a target, not only was it like an old fashioned wiretap, but he could also pinpoint her location with the GPS in it.

It was time to make contact with the target Gabriel thought. He had to return her lost items and find a way into that house to plant other surveillance equipment. Once completed, it would only take a few days to study her routine before the hit.

Chapter 4
New Neighbors

Finding the right opportunity to get to know your target usually had to be planned out methodically, but for a teenage girl it was all too easy. Once Gabriel saw her outside washing her car he decided that it was time. Grabbing her belongings and walking to the door he heard Alex mention something behind him that sounded like *try not to stare at her chest, she hates guys that do that.* With a smile, Gabriel opened the door and walked out.

Halfway across the street Gabriel could see that the girl was dressed in shorts and a red bikini top. *Great, how do I not look at the chest of a nineteen year old girl in a bikini?* Gabriel kept his focus on the red Ford Mustang that she was washing.

Cady was squatted trying to clean the mud out of her hubcaps when she saw a boy walking toward her. *Great she thought, another guy that saw me in a bathing suit and now wants in my pants,* she thought. Even though she knew she was attractive, Cady was insecure about the guys that wanted to date her simply because she was hot. That is why she had not been in a relationship since she entered high school. That had been almost four years ago. Graduating this summer had been like a huge weight had been lifted off of her chest. She hoped that by going to a good college the guys there would not be so critical about who they dated and what they looked like, but that was wishful thinking on her part.

The boy crossed over onto the lawn and slowed his walk. Looking toward Cady, he cracked a smile; one that even Cady thought was cute.

"Can I help you," she said in a loud tone so the boy could hear.

"I hope so," said the boy as he picked up the pace again.

"By the look of your driver's license you are Cady Bishop."

Cady practically sprinted to the boy, overjoyed that the contents of her purse were being returned. Stopping just short of the boy before tackling him like a pro football star, she quickly grabbed the contents of her purse and looked through it. Everything seemed to be here; Wallet, credit cards, driver's license and cell phone. Cady quickly looked up with a look of inquisitiveness.

"Where did you find my stuff?"

"Didn't your friend Jan tell you, my Brother Alex found it at the mall and texted her that he had it."

Still looking intently at the boy, she could usually tell a liar by the way that they looked at her, but this guy was dead serious, looking straight into her eyes with that smile she has seen from across the lawn.

"Thank you so much for bringing it back, I can't get by without my cell."

"It was really no problem, we just moved in across the street and I saw you out here, so I thought I had better return it sooner rather than later."

"I appreciate that, it means a lot that you brought it over."

Cady looked the boy over, he guessed he was about 18-19, 150 pounds, dark brown hair; then it hit her, his eyes were the same bright green as hers. All of the people she had ever known didn't have eyes like this.

"Your eyes," she said in a hushed tone.

"Yea, same color huh. Name's Gabriel Mason," he said as he lifted his hand to shake hers.

Cady did the same, and as they shook hands, she could not help but stare into his eyes again. She had read that the color of their eyes were a one in five million chance. Go figure that he would move in across the street from her.

"How old are you Gabe?"

"I'm twenty three"

"Wow, I would have guessed nineteen at the most."

"I hear that a lot."

Cady and Gabriel sat on her front porch for nearly an hour talking about his move from Las Vegas Nevada, what kind of car he drove, favorite movies and so on. Cady was impressed that he liked the same type of movies, and had the same taste in food. He was well dressed with a black shirt, blue jeans and black leather jacket. He was very well built, all muscle from what she could tell.

When it was time for Cady to meet Jan at their local coffee shop, she almost didn't want to go. Not once did Gabriel stare at her or ogle her chest. He seemed like the perfect guy, smart, funny and good looking. She decided that she could not stand up Jan, so she stood up trying to give a signal that it was time to go. Gabriel was very perceptive and noticed the signal, standing up and walking in front of her off the front porch.

"I'll be home in an hour or so, but I have to meet my friend for coffee."

"That's cool; I have to get some work done anyway. By the way is your mother or father home, I would like to meet them to let them know about moving in across the street."

Cady walked down toward her car and opened the door before turning back to Gabriel.

"My mom died last year of cancer, and my dad is at work, he won't be home until tomorrow at the earliest."

"I'm sorry to hear about your mom. My parents passed away in a car accident last year, that's why Alex and I moved out here. Vegas was just too much of a reminder of them."

Cady thought that it was the perfect time to leave and climbed into her car, closing the door and firing up the engine, she rolled down the window and smiling at Gabriel, she said something that he really didn't expect.

"I hope this is the start of a long friendship Gabe."

You have no idea, he thought.

Chapter 5
Random Acts of Chance

Walking into Rachel's, the local coffee shop, Cady spotted Jan in her usual seat. A small table near the fireplace on the right wall. Grabbing her usual coffee from the counter, a Caramel Macchiato, she walked to Jan's table and sat. She recounted to Jan about meeting Gabriel and all of the things they had in common.

"Why didn't you tell me that Alex had my stuff, I called the police and filed a stolen property complaint."

"Oops," was all that Jan could muster.

"Well, anyway, it's nice to have my stuff back."

The girls sat and chatted about the day's events and continued to drink their coffee. Jan recounted all of the text messages she had gotten from Alex, and about how much they had in common also. Cady began to get a little suspicious of how these brothers were different from each other, and yet, had so much in common with each of the girls. Cady decided to blow off that train of thought because it was refreshing to be able to talk about guys they were interested in.

Before either of the girls could get off the topic of the boys, Cady's cell phone rang. She removed it from her purse and looked at the Caller ID,

"DAD". Cady opened the phone and struck up a conversation with her father.

"Hi Daddy!"

"Hello honey, everything ok."

"Yea, why?"

"Just checking in, you know how fathers worry."

Cady knew all too well how fathers worry, especially hers. Once when she tried to ride her bicycle for the first time without the training wheels and fell, he had put them back on and made her use them until she was twelve years old. Try explaining that to your friends!

"I'm at the coffee shop with Jan; we were just talking about a couple of boys we met."

"Honey, I thought we talked about this, no boys right now, it's dangerous out there."

Cady had heard this one too many times. He never wanted her to date; in fact, he is another reason why she didn't date in high school.

"Daddy, I know what we talked about but I'm nineteen years old. I need to get out there and date before I shrivel up and die. Besides, you would like this guy, he and his brother moved in across the street and he came over to meet you."

"Came to meet me? How old are they?"

"Gabriel is twenty three, and Alex is eighteen."

"And which one are you interested in honey?"

"Gabriel," Cady said shyly.

"Honey, I have to go, we can talk about this tomorrow night when I get home."

"Fine, bye," Cady said shutting her phone.

Looking around the coffee shop she had not noticed Jan go back to the counter for another coffee. *Jan is a weird one, drinking strait black coffee,* she thought. Once Jan had gotten her refill, she sat back at the table and Cady recounted what had transpired over the phone. Midway through her story, she could tell that Jan was no longer paying attention to her; instead her focus was on the counter to the left. Cady looked over and saw Alex who already had coffee in hand and was waiting for his change. Like he knew where the girls were sitting he walked over and pulled a chair from another table and sat on the side of the two person table.

"What are the chances, I find a new coffee shop, and two pretty girls sitting here all alone," he said with a smile.

Alex pulled out a chair and sat with the girls. He knew that Jan had a teenage crush on him and thought about exploiting her for information on Cady but decided against it. *Great, I'm one of the only assassins with an angel on my shoulder telling me not to do cruel things.* He knew that killing people was cruel too, but figured he modeled himself more after the movie "Wanted." *Kill one save a thousand,* he thought as he chuckled to himself. It was true however; he never knew the repercussions of letting someone live once they had been targeted. Perhaps if letting a target live, they would kill other innocent people and that is something he could never let happen. Gabriel was the same way, never taking a job that would take innocent casualties.

The girls chatted with Alex about the day's events, and he was already starting to get bored. He decided to raise the stakes of the conversation by bringing up Gabriel.

"So my brother seems to like you Cady. It's odd; he has never taken interest in a girl since our parents died last year."

Cady looked a little distraught and Alex thought he might have blown it for a second, but then a small smile crept across her face and he knew that she was glad he had said something.

"I'm sorry to hear about your parents Alex," said Jan.

"It's cool, they would have wanted us to move on and I have for the most part, its Gabriel that is still taking it pretty hard."

"What happened, if you don't mind me asking," said Jan.

"They were killed in a car accident. It was raining and my dad lost control of the car. They hit a tree and were killed instantly."

"Oh my god," said Cady looking horrified.

"We are coming up on one year since their death on Saturday. I can't imagine that Gabriel will be very talkative."

Cady looked at Jan with a smile. They appeared to be thinking the same thing, but Alex was clearly confused.

"So we take his mind off of it, said Cady.

"What do you mean," asked Alex.

"Lets take him out, get his mind off of things."

Alex was glad that Cady had taken the lead with the idea. It would be much easier to take her to some random location, put two in the back of her head and dump the body.

"I don't know girls, I'm not sure he will be into going out."

"Well we will kidnap him and force him to have a good time," retorted Jan.

"Well you have four days to plan something, and count me in," said Alex.

With a smile, the only thought running through his head was *JACKPOT.*

Chapter 6
Home Invasion

The plan to have Alex stall the girls at the coffee shop seems to have paid off, Gabriel thought as he walked across the lawn of the Bishop residence. Walking around to the back he saw an in ground pool, a three car garage, and quite possibly the largest barbecue pit he had ever seen. Creeping slowly to the back door and pulling out a lock pick kit that he liked to keep handy for just such an occasion, he quickly had the back door open and was entering the house.

Knowing the floor plan is always a good idea when entering a house. If you're lucky, you will already know exactly where to place the listening devices and video equipment. Moving to the living room Gabriel pulled a chair toward the smoke detector on the ceiling. Removing the cover and placing in on the seat of the chair he took a listening device from his pack and placed it under the speaker. This would be able to pick up any sound in the room, even if at a whisper. Before replacing the cover he removed the battery and inserted a new one. Gabriel had a habit of doing this as one of his previous targets had to replace the battery to get his smoke detector to stop chirping and found one of his bugs.

Next Gabriel moved to the phones and inserted a bug in each of them.

Unfortunately, it was hard to tell if the father would know to check the phones for a tap but it is a risk one must take. Next he placed a small video camera and microphone in the central air ducts on the ceilings for a full 360 degree view.

The last place Gabriel had to set up equipment was Cady's bedroom. Moving up the stairs and taking a left at the top he found her room on the far end of the hall. He opened the door and walked inside to scout the best place for his bugs. Finding no spot to hide a camera he decided to drill into the white drywall of her room and insert one there. After placing the camera, he found a matching color screen to fit over the lens so that it blended with the walls. Cady or her father would never know the camera was there if they were more than six inches from it.

Gabriel moved to plant a microphone in the headboard. Taking a piece of plastic tape he fastened it under the top of the headboard and tested the microphone for a clear signal. Looking at her desk, Gabriel decided to plant a virus in Cady's laptop. This virus was genius, Alex had invented the capability to not only see what keystrokes were taking place, but they were able to view exactly what was on the screen and even activate the built in webcam for a clear view of her surroundings if she were to go mobile. He quickly downloaded the contents of her laptop and was ready to leave.

Testing a small handheld device he had pulled from his pack, Gabriel was downstairs before he knew it. The device, a small detonator, would set off a harmless charge when the job was complete destroying the equipment he had planted here.

Soon, the girl would be dead, and he would be on a plane back to New York for his debriefing. Leaving the way he came, Gabriel went back out through the back yard and made his way back to the apartment. He was ready, he thought. This job is just too easy.

Gabriel returned to the apartment and powered on the surveillance equipment to test their operation. Everything seemed to be in working order. Proud of himself he opened his laptop and uploaded the contents of Cady's computer to his screen.

Gabriel was examining the contents of Cady's laptop with no luck of finding any information of why she was marked for termination. Cady had everything a girl should have on a nineteen year old girl's laptop. A link to her Facebook account showed photos of Cady with her friends. She seemed like an average girl. Gabriel was not supposed to ask why, just do, which always pissed him off. This girl was different, innocent. Next he checked her bank account which was fairly normal for a girl her age. Automatic deposits into her account every week from her father, almost like an allowance, debit card transactions, and cash withdrawals were the only things on this account. Gabriel would have guessed to see a very large deposit or withdrawal being the reason she was in such trouble, but there was nothing over one hundred dollars over the past year.

Checking her documents revealed nothing unusual either, but playing a hunch he opened the options menu and displayed any hidden objects on the computer. One previously hidden Microsoft Word document caught his eye; it was marked "For my eyes only." Opening the file, Gabriel knew he had just found a sort of computerized diary.

The first entry was logged when Cady was only sixteen. He decided that this may give some clue as to why she was now worth his attention.

December 19th, 2007

Dear Diary,

God I hate that phrase. In the future, this is a reminder never to start with dear diary again. My father just bought me this laptop for school. I have wanted one forever! This is the coolest thing! I can't wait to get my room hooked up to the internet so that I can talk to my friends on here. Everyone I know has a computer to keep in touch and now I can too. Till next time!

Gabriel was dumbfounded at the entries. These entries were more innocent than the girl looked. Deciding to skip a little farther ahead, he found one dated slightly more recent.

April 24th, 2010

I cannot wait to get out of this hell hole of a school. These guys who try to hit on me all the time are ridiculous. I can't walk ten steps without being asked to the prom. I wanted to go with Joey but seeing as how he was in a car accident with his father and can't walk, I guess that's out. Frank asked me out on a date this Saturday, but I'm really not interested. He is good looking, but can't seem to stop checking me out. I am so tired of a guy not being able to look me in the eye. Guys my age are just worried about having sex with me. I want someone who likes me for who I am, not what I look like.

May 5th, 2010

My father has just returned from his trip to China. He said his friend Clay had been mugged over there and died. What a terrible thing o happen to anyone. I can't imagine what Clay's family is feeling right now but I am so sorry for them.

Since Dad got home, he is acting really distant. I can't blame him though, just losing a friend and all. He is so paranoid that I will get mugged now that I can't leave the house until he says it's ok. Some business trip that turned out to be. All it really did for him was make him scared of every shadow in the house. I think there is something he is not telling me and I intend to find out what.

This was it! Gabriel knew exactly why the girl was being targeted. He never figured that the father would be involved with the Chinese but it made perfect sense. The Triads were one bunch of people you don't want piss off. Not only do they come for you, but they will kill your entire family and make you watch before they put a bullet in your head. *This girl is innocent,* he thought, completely innocent. He was sent to kill a nineteen year old girl because her father ticked off some triads.

Gabriel heard the sound of keys being dropped on the hardwood floor of the hallway, which was the signal that it was just Alex. The door opened and in walked his partner with a smile from ear to ear.

"What are you grinning at?"

"Nothing," Alex retorted putting on a serious face.

Alex could tell something was wrong with Gabriel because he didn't make eye contact. He just kept staring at his laptop intently.

"What's wrong?"

Gabriel turned to Alex with a look of pity.

"This girl; she didn't do anything wrong," said Gabriel.

"How do you know that?"

"It was her father all along. He pissed off some Triads, or someone that knew them, and now they are going to kill the girl, then her father."

Gabriel recounted the journal entry on the girl's computer. Alex sat motionless, listening to the story, with a look of understanding at the situation. Gabriel recounted the trip to China, the death of Martin Bishop's partner and the paranoia for his daughter when he returned home.

"It does make sense," Alex concluded.

"What I don't understand is why the Choir would send us? We have been working together for three years and have never silenced a target that wasn't guilty of some heinous crime. Marcus knows I don't work like this."

"Yea, we are assassins with a conscience," Alex quipped.

"Listen Gabriel, we can't just drop the job. This is what we are paid to do, somebody needs killin, we kill"em. The best we can do for them is to make it quick and painless. If we don't do the job, the Choir will send someone else to finish it and then send them to finish us too."

Gabriel knew that he was telling the truth, the Choir does not look favorably on failure. The last agent to not silence his target was Sammial. He found his target, had a knife to his throat, and then for some reason did not go through with the kill. The Choir had sent Gabriel for him and that had always weighed heavily on him. Gabriel located the agent in Louisiana, marched him to a secluded spot in the forest and drove a knife into his heart. He never asked Sammial why he didn't kill the man; he just did as he was instructed to.

Chapter 7
The Almost Ex

Two days of surveillance was enough to drive anyone mad. Sitting in a reclining chair, staring both out the window and into the monitors were strangely tiring. Gabriel fought sleep as he continued to monitor the girl. She had been on her computer surfing the internet for nearly two hours now. Gabriel shrugged off using his laptop to see what she was doing an hour ago. Reading the news, posting random messages to friends on Facebook, and then settling in to watch a movie on Netflix. *This girl really loves her computer*, he thought.

It was nearly midnight when Gabriel spied someone walking down the street. He pulled his night vision scope out of its case and recognized the face of the boy from the file he had been reading. James Sullivan lived just two blocks away, and always had something to say to Cady, but usually called her on the cell phone that she constantly had stuck in her ear.

The boy walked into her front yard and froze approximately three feet from where he entered. Pulling out his cell phone and dialing a number, Gabriel knew there was only one number he could be dialing. Gabriel looked at his dummy phone and saw it light up with the caller ID reading "Barf". Gabriel laughed to himself. It was obvious that Cady had no love for this guy, and yet he tried to get her on a date every night. Gabriel picked up the cell phone when he saw it stop flashing and turn a solid color of blue meaning that Cady had answered.

"Hi James."

"Hey beautiful, guess where I am."

"Where?"

"Outside in your yard."

A long silence from Cady indicated that she was not pleased to hear the news.

"Why are you outside James."

"I wanted to talk to you in person, it's important."

Another long pause and the phone went dead. Two minutes later Cady appeared in the front doorway of her house. Slipping on her sandals, Gabriel prepared his listening device that looked more like a satellite on a stick. He plugged in the ear phones and began listening.

"James you can't keep doing this, I don't want to go on a date with you."

"Hey beautiful, I didn't come here for a date."

"You didn't?"

Gabriel sat motionless eavesdropping on the conversation. Pulling out his silenced rifle from under the recliner, he positioned it on the open window. *I could take her right now and make it look like the boy did it,* he thought. He decided against the hit and continued to listen.

"I was just out with some friends and wanted to stop by for a goodnight kiss."

"You have got to be kidding me. James, your drunk! If I don't want to date you, what makes you think that I want to kiss you?"

"Come on beaut—"

"Stop saying that," she yelled.

Gabriel now has the rifle pointing directly at James and had his finger on the trigger. *One shot between the shoulder blades would be sufficient,* he thought, but decided against it. Instead, Gabriel lowered his silenced rifle to the floor and stood up from the chair. Taking a silenced pistol from its holster on the back of the chair and tucking it into his back waistband he walked straight out the door.

Cady was extremely agitated that this boy would come here not only drunk, but try to throw himself on her. She had told him for the last time to stop but James obviously wasn't getting the hint. He moved in closer to Cady, close enough to get a hand around her shoulder and pull her close. Cady struggled but James was stronger. He continued to hold her close to him, then leaned in for a kiss. Cady knew of only one way to break the news to James and really get her message across. She reached and kicked as hard as she could; her foot catching James in the crotch.

James fell backward in obvious pain. Cady could see the instant anger on his face, and getting up much faster than she thought possible, he grabbed her by the front of her shirt and reached up with his right hand and balled it into a fist. Cady grimaced and looked away expecting a solid blow to her face. Instead, James's had fell away from her shirt and before she could turn back around, she heard a loud thud and the sound of James hitting the ground hard.

Turning to look at what had just happened she found Gabriel standing in front of her and the tall form of James laying face up in the grass.

"Are you ok," asked Gabriel.

"Yea, I'm fine," was all Cady could muster.

Regaining her composure was not easy, and when she finally got up the courage to survey the damage she found herself still shocked at James lying on the ground. She kept her distance from James and tried to see where Gabriel had come from. It was as if he appeared out of nowhere. She replayed the scene in her head over and over and figured that she had only looked away for a second before Gabriel had appeared.

James was now struggling to his feet and Gabriel moved to stand in front of Cady. Taking a defensive position all she could see was the already bruised face of James staring with absolute hatred toward Gabriel.

"What are you the new boyfriend?"

"You could say that," said Gabriel.

Cady, still amazed that Gabriel who was only 5'10 facing off against James, who played football all throughout high school and was now on a full ride to Texas A&M as a lineman. James stood 6'5" and was easily 250 pounds. Gabriel did not look scared however, he stood his ground between Cady and James.

"You got a lucky shot man, but let's see how good you are when I can see you coming."

Gabriel looked disgusted, almost as if James stood no chance, which Cady would have thought the opposite. Gabriel was certainly not built to be a fighter, but Cady now knew that he must be pretty good at it. Looking at the boy, Gabriel said something that made Cady's heart beat even faster than before.

"I'll make you a deal, turn around and walk away, and I won't have to kill you."

Kill him, she thought. This guy will take Gabriel apart then come for me. She ran through their future fight several times in her head and could see no way of Gabriel winning against this humongous guy.

"Kill me huh, you know who I am?"

"You talk too much," was Gabriel's response.

With that comment James moved in to throw a punch at Gabriel. Swinging with his left, he caught only air as he stumbled forward. Cady looked for Gabriel and found him standing behind the hulking football player. James turned around and took another swing and still never saw Gabriel step to the side and let him fly right past. Cady was amazed at Gabriel's speed; one minute he was standing there as if ready to take a punch and the next was standing beside James not even fighting back.

"Do you really want to do this," Gabriel asked.

"Do I really want to kick your ass; yea I think I really do," said James in an obvious drunken stupor.

James rushed at Gabriel again but this time he didn't move. James threw three punches in rapid succession at Gabriel but they were only brushed aside like they were nothing. Gabriel then moved inside of the reach of James's arms and threw a punch of his own landing right between his eyes. Stumbling back with a look of pure surprise, James regained his composure and came again.

"Time to end this," said Gabriel silent enough that only Cady could hear.

Spinning backward in a 360 movement, Gabriel lifted his left leg and placed it perfectly on the side of James's face knocking him to the ground once more.

James lay motionless on the ground yet again and Cady ran to Gabriel throwing her arms out and latching onto him in a hug.

"Thank you so much. I thought he was really going to hurt me."

Gabriel returned the embrace to Cady stroking her long brown hair with his hand.

"He won't hurt you while I'm around."

Gabriel looked serene with only compassion on his face. Cady knew that she wanted to kiss him, but the embrace did not last long enough, Gabriel pulled away and moved back toward the street looking up and down, checking for cars.

"What are you doing," she asked.

"Checking for the police."

"Why," she asked in bewilderment.

"I called them five minutes ago when I was walking across the street."

Cady was still in disbelief that Gabriel had managed to stop James so easily. Also looking up and down the street, she could see no cars on the road.

Another five minutes later the police finally arrived. Cady could see that it was Sheriff Jon Faulk climbing out of the driver's seat. As the sheriff meandered over to Gabriel and asked what was going on Cady was too far out of earshot to hear the first part of the conversation. Closing the gap between them she heard Gabriel recounting the story of what had just transpired outside of her house.

"After I called you, this guy was raised his arm to hit her and I came up behind him and put a stop to it."

"This true ma'am," asked the Sheriff now looking at Cady.

"Yes, he tried to hit me. Gabriel lives across the street came over just in time."

"That so," said the Sheriff looking back at Gabriel.

"Yea, I called before this happened, I didn't expect the guy to attack her or myself, but I didn't want the girl to be hurt."

The girl, Cady thought. *How can he just call me the girl when he knows my name?* It bewildered her at the thought of what Gabriel meant by what he had just said, but she was quickly put to rest when Gabriel turned and winked at her.

The Sheriff, still looking angry from being woken out of bed, walked over to James and started to pick the boy up.

"Come on big fella, you need to sleep this off."

As the Sheriff helped James keep his balance on his way to the car, he stopped in front of Gabriel and Cady.

"Either of you want to press charges?"

"No," they both said in succession.

With that, the Sheriff continued to tote James to the squad car and placed him in the back seat. Climbing back into his car, the Sheriff sped off.

Gabriel walked back to Cady with another compassionate look on his face.

"Looks like you have had a long night."

"Looks that way," Cady said mustering a faint smile.

"Alright, you go get some rest and I'll come see how you're doing tomorrow."

Cady nodded and silently turned toward her house and began walking. Gabriel stood still until she reached her door. Cady turned around and gave Gabriel an inquisitive look.

"Can you teach me," she asked.

Gabriel knew what she was talking about but decided to play dumb.

"Teach you what?"

"How to fight like you do."

Gabriel smiled a reassuring smile.

"Maybe, but first you need some rest."

"Ok," Cady said before turning and closing the door behind her.

Gabriel turned and walked toward his apartment and began walking home. *That guy could nearly have done the job for me, why didn't I just let him beat her,* he wondered to himself. He decided that thinking was too overrated tonight and silently trekked across the street home.

Chapter 8
Company

Alex awoke to a knock on the door. Crawling out of bed and grabbing a 9mm berretta from the nightstand, he quickly moved out of the bedroom and down the hallway. When he reached the living room, he saw Gabriel asleep on the recliner. Alex checked his watch and realized that he was late for his shift. Gabriel typically lets Alex sleep but it appears as if he gave up waiting for him and passed out.

Another knock on the door was Alex's cue to check the surveillance equipment they had placed in the hallway for security. *It was much better to look at a camera feed than take the risk of being shot through the door,* he thought. Alex tapped the TAB key on the laptop sitting near Gabriel and saw someone he truly did not expect.

A quick double take to make sure he was not still dreaming and it was confirmed. Cady stood on the other side of the door moving her arm up for a third knock. He ran to the door and opened it far enough that the chain on the door clicked to its maximum length.

"Hi Cady," Alex said with a nervous tone in his voice.

"Hey, is Gabriel here, I wanted to thank him again for last night."

"Last night?"

"He didn't tell you, he saved me from a guy that was creeping around my place."

Alex now looked at his sleeping partner wondering what he was thinking. *Saved her, he could have let whoever it was kill her and we would be done with this mess,* he thought.

"Cady, give me a minute to put on a shirt and I'll let you in."

"Ok," she said.

Alex lied of course; he just wanted time to clean the apartment so it looked a lot less like a stakeout. Running to the kitchen he scrapped all of the ammunition they had laid out into a black duffel bag then threw it into the closet in the hallway. Now taking the laptop and shutting down the surveillance system, he made the computer look as if Gabriel fell asleep while looking at Facebook. Taking Gabriel's rifle and shoving it into the closet where he had thrown the ammo a few seconds ago he now ran to put on a shirt and let Cady in. Finding a short sleeve button up shirt in his suitcase, he quickly threw it on and ran back to the door.

Removing the chain from the door and opening it he saw Cady standing where she had been before. Wearing a pink spaghetti strap top and blue jeans she entered the apartment looking around as if she knew that something was out of place. Alex looked at her wondering if she had heard him moving their equipment but quickly dismissed the thought. It was almost as if she was looking for something he missed. Turning to Alex she looked at him with a hopeful smile.

"So where's Gabe?"

Alex had never heard anyone call his partner Gabe before. It was kind of fitting once he thought about it. Turning toward the recliner Alex pointed to his sleeping partner.

"Sleepy head is still passed out," said Alex.

"Well he did have a big night. I didn't sleep very well, I kept thinking of everything that had happened. He really did save me Alex, you should have seen him."

"I'll make some coffee and you can tell me about it since I seem to have missed all the fun."

Alex moved into the kitchen and poured some water into the coffee pot. Putting several scoops of coffee into the filter and dumping the water into the back of the machine took only a minute. In that time Cady just sat at the kitchen table and stared at Gabriel in his recliner.

"Pretty amazing isn't he," said Cady.

"He's one of kind," muttered Alex.

"I wonder what was going through his head when he fought James. I can't believe that he managed to beat him, let alone do it without ever getting hit."

Alex knew if this were some regular person around town that Gabriel would have no problem kicking his ass without even breaking a sweat but he decided to keep his mouth shut.

"So tell me what happened last night. I can't believe I missed all the excitement."

Cady recounted the events of last night beginning with receiving the unwanted phone call to going outside to try and make the guy leave. She was fascinated how Gabriel appeared out of nowhere and stopped the boy from hitting her.

"It was as if he just appeared," she said.

Alex knew that Gabriel was excellent at concealing himself until he was close enough to act. It was a trick he had picked up from Michael, who could just step out of a shadow as if he had been there all along.

Alex stood up from the table and poured the coffee, placing a teaspoon of Sugar in his along with some milk, and in Cady's cup he just added the milk. Sitting back own and handing the cup to Cady, she looked up in amazement.

"How did you know I only take milk?"

Alex could have slapped himself. A huge mistake like that can blow your cover in an instant.

"Doesn't every girl hate sugar in their coffee?"

Looking down at her cup, still thinking that it was a bit odd for Alex to know how she drank her coffee.

"I guess so," she said.

Alex decided to use this opportunity to try and figure out what this girl knew in terms of being targeted. He assumed if she knew anything now would be the best time to come clean, especially to someone near her age.

"So what other kind of trouble have you gotten yourself into these days?"

"What do you mean, Cady retorted."

"I mean, are there any other guys chasing after you that we should know about or is there something else that will put you in danger?"

Cady appeared to be thinking long and hard about the question. Alex thought it was odd that she would not come right out and talk to him about any troubling situations since that seemed to be what girls liked to talk about these days.

"I can't think of anything else."

Alex thought she might be lying, but her eyes were telling the truth. Completely dumbfounded, he trailed off into the living room and shook Gabriel's chair to wake him. She is a tough nut to crack, but Alex suspected that she knew absolutely nothing about being marked for termination. Shaking his fake brother's chair again, Gabriel shot up ready for a fight. Alex placed a hand on Gabriel's shoulder and silently reassured him that they were not under attack. Gabriel always was a bit jumpy when it came to waking him up.

Gabriel looked around the apartment realizing that their equipment was shut off and his weapons were nowhere to be found. Taking another look he saw Cady sitting in the kitchen drinking her coffee and smiling in his direction. Gabriel rose from his recliner and proceeded to the kitchen area to meet his guest.

"What brings you over here," he asked.

Cady looked shy but quickly shrugged that off. She got out of her chair and walked toward Gabriel. She wrapped her arms around him for another hug and held him for a few seconds. Looking up at him without breaking her embrace, she almost looked as if she were going to cry.

"I wanted to thank you again for last night. I thought James was really going to hurt me."

Gabriel looked deep into her eyes and could tell that the girl was still scared. *This is not the way that someone acts if they knew that they were in bigger trouble than having a high school football player try to slam his fist into her face*, he thought.

"Cady, really, it was no problem. I just wanted to help."

"Well, you didn't have to, and I am grateful that you did."

Cady finally broke away from Gabriel looking as if she were

embarrassed for holding her embrace for so long. She was amazed that Gabriel himself did not try to push her way. From what she had learned of him from Alex, he really did not like being so close to someone.

Gabriel moved to the coffee pot and poured himself a drink. Sipping on the steaming coffee he looked back at Alex who was making kissing faces behind Cady's back. For a second he thought about throwing the coffee cup and hitting him in the face with it, but the moment passed. Gabriel looked back at Cady and she was still staring at him.

"So what else can I do for you? Anyone else need a beating? Mailman, other ex boyfriends perhaps?"

Cady laughed, obviously amused at what Gabriel had said. Gabriel had really not seen the girl laugh before; smile yes, but never laugh.

"He wasn't my boyfriend, just some guy that thought he could get into my pants. But you did say that you would teach me some moves today Gabe, and I'm holding you to it."

Gabriel had remembered her turning toward him last night before going into her house and asking the question.

"Alright, when do you want to get started?"

"No time like the present," she said with a smile.

Chapter 9
Self Defense

Cady and Gabriel stood outside her house in the front yard. Gabriel looked at the spot where James had been dragged away by the Sheriff and chuckled to himself. Cady was now wearing a pink tank top shirt and a pair of her tight jeans.

"So what first," she asked.

"First, I am going to teach you how to get away from someone who is attacking you."

Cady looked slightly disappointed, he suspected that she wanted to learn how to fight first so Gabriel decided to put a spin on his teachings to make her feel better.

"Don't worry; these moves I am going to show you will also hurt your attacker a lot."

Cady perked up at the thought and came bounding over to Gabriel. Looking as innocent as ever, Gabriel knew with enough time, he could even teach her how to be an assassin; although it did not appear that she would be capable of killing anyone.

"The first thing I want you to do is grab my by the shirt with one hand and try to punch me with the other, like James did to you last night."

Before attacking Gabriel, Cady reached up and tightened her pony tail so her hair would not fall into her face. She then walked over to Gabriel and placed her left hand on his shirt and balled it up into a fist holding him in place. She then raised her right arm as if she were going to hit him in the face.

"What now," she asked.

"Now you're going to hit me."

"Seriously?"

"Cady, if you want to learn how to defend yourself, there is only one way, defend against an attacker when it really counts."

Cady looked as if she didn't want to hit him, but with the moves she saw yesterday she guessed that she had no chance of actually landing a punch. In slow motion she moved her fist to his face. Gabriel stood in place until her fist was resting on his cheek.

"So are you going to hit me now," he asked with a coy smile.

"Alright, I'll try and hit you."

She raised her arm again and this time swung her fist as hard as she could at Gabriel. A second before the punch landed Gabriel had moved behind her.

"How did you do that?"

Gabriel smiled and placed his hand on her shirt, and came in with a punch. Stopping just short of her face, he held his position and began directing her through the movements.

"I want you to take my hand that is holding your shirt and twist it to the right. This can incapacitate the person immediately if done correctly. Then, when my fist in close to where I am going to hit you, I want you to raise your right arm and block it with your forearm. Once you do that, I want you to duck, and I will move right past you."

Cady did as she was instructed and after a couple of attempts she got it right. They practiced the same move over and over, each time Gabriel came at her faster so that she would get the idea of being in a real fight. Finally, once they had practiced the move enough, Gabriel began teaching her how to escape from choke holds, hair pulls and bear hugs.

Gabriel was impressed at how fast Cady was picking up these moves. It took Gabriel weeks to learn what she had just done in an hour. Gabriel now began teaching Cady how to fight back, throwing punches and kicks. He taught her the basics of what she needed to survive, such as the forward punch, roundhouse kick, and many other variations. Cady had immediately realized that this was not just street smarts, Gabriel had been in the martial arts.

"Where did you learn this stuff?"

"My friend Michael taught me everything I know about fighting."

It was odd calling another assassin a friend, but Michael and Alex really were considered friends in his mind. Michael had taken Gabriel under his wing when he made level two in the Choir, and had learned more from him that he ever had in levels five through three.

Gabriel knew that teaching Cady to defend herself against an attacker was not the best idea, since he was supposed to kill her, but she would stand no chance against a member of the Choir. In his mind, this girl had suffered enough over the petty things in life; a father who was never there, and crazy guys that would try to hurt her once they had been rejected. This in his mind was a way to help her die happy. He had considered not fulfilling the contract on her life, but that would spell death for himself and his partner.

Gabriel decided to show Cady some throwing techniques before their lesson ended. Several variations of the easy ones would come in handy for any situation where your attacker was close. He first showed her the reap, which consisted of throwing someone off balance and taking their feet out from under them. Then he decided to show her a slightly more advanced move called the reverse hip throw. A couple of tries and she did not have it right, which Gabriel suspected meant that she was getting tired.

"I don't think I'll get this one, it's pretty complicated."

"You'll be fine, practice is all it takes to prefect these moves. Remember that in a real fight, if your heart rate elevates too high, you will forget up to sixty percent of what you know due to your elevated adrenaline level."

"So, do this move on me Gabe, I think I can learn better by seeing it done."

Gabriel obliged and wrapped one arm around her stomach and began to toss her over his back. When she was directly over him he stopped and began to explain the physics of this throw and how damaging it could be.

"This way, it is impossible to defend against this throw once they have reached this point," said Gabriel."

"I know a way out of this one," Cady whispered excitedly.

"You think so? I urge you to try anything to get me to drop you before you crash onto your head."

Cady, beamed a big smile that Gabriel could not see, but knew she had something in mind. Cady reached down with her right hand and began tickling Gabriel's right side. Gabriel was in such shock that he collapsed with Cady landing on top of him. Lying on the ground together they began laughing uncontrollably.

"Well, I guess if your attacker is ticklish then you have nothing to worry about," laughed Gabriel.

As they lay on the ground still laughing about Cady's brilliant counter attack, a black Cadillac Escalade pulled into the driveway and stopped. Cady and Gabriel lay motionless waiting to see who had just pulled in. On the other side of the vehicle they heard a door open and slam shut. As the vehicle began to back out of the driveway, they saw Martin Bishop standing in the driveway with his hands on his hips staring at Cady.

Gabriel was the first to jump up as if he were in trouble, but knew it was the right thing to do. When a man sees his daughter lying in the grass with a stranger, it can look a great deal more suspicious than most things.

Martin approached Cady and Gabriel quickly. With a sour look on his face he stopped just short of Cady and looked as if he would give her the third degree.

"Young lady, I thought you said you would be safe while I was gone."

"I am, thanks to Gabriel," she retorted in a huff.

"Thanks to…"

"Me," Gabriel chimed in. "My name is Gabriel Mason, my brother and I just moved in across the street. It is good to finally meet you Mr. Bishop."

Martin shot a very unsure glance to Cady then turned his attention back to Gabriel. Seeming to size him up as no threat, and motioned for Gabriel to follow him across the lawn without Cady.

"So you're the boy my daughter has been talking about. I'm glad she found a friend Mr. Mason, but what she doesn't need is another boy chasing her around like a lost puppy. I have been very disappointed in the boys that have called on her in the past, and I want to assure you that no-one will ever hurt my daughter mentally or physically."

For a second Gabriel thought that Bishop was onto him. *What did he mean physically, does he think we are the ones that were sent to kill her? Of course he would be right, but I have given no information for him to believe that.*

Gabriel shook off the warning from Bishop as if it were a warning he gives everyone around his daughter.

"Mr. Bishop, I hope that you don't think that I mean any harm to Cady. If you do, I will respect the wishes of her father; go back across the street, and leave you and your daughter alone."

Gabriel thought he may have laid it on a bit thick, but he wanted to come across as the most gentle and respectful individual that Martin Bishop had ever met.

"Don't get me wrong son, I am just a little on edge, I hope that I didn't scare you away from being friends with my daughter. It does after all seem like she really values your friendship, I just worry about her."

"Mr. Bishop, I value Cady's friendship as well. With the loss of our parents last year, my brother and I have not been very social. In fact, Cady is the first friend I have made since they died."

Bishop still looked unsure of the boy. Gabriel thought it was the fatherly need to protect his daughter. *I guess you should trust your gut Mr. Bishop; I am here to kill your daughter after all.*

Chapter 10
Intrusion

Gabriel sat watching the monitors of the Bishops home. He studied all corners, shelves and rooms looking for a place to hide in the shadows for his kill. Killing Cady would be the hardest mission Gabriel had ever undertaken. Not for the reason that she was dangerous, but exactly the opposite. Gabriel had never killed an innocent human being before. All of his targets in the past were men who had committed some violent crime or political figures that liked to rape little girls, like his last target.

Cady and her father had left their home to go out to eat together. Not the most ideal situation for surveillance, but he trusted Alex to follow them without being seen. Looking deeper into the screen Gabriel noticed movement in the house. A small shadow swept across the living room and onto the stairs. Gabriel watched the screen intently but saw nothing else. Deciding that the monitors were not just enough he opened the menu on his laptop and activated the motion sensors in the house.

Cady was always tasked with activating the alarm system when leaving the house, but she nearly always forgot about it. Safety is just never on the mind of a nineteen year old girl, especially since she had no idea that people were out to kill her. Gabriel diverted his attention back to the laptop and was reading a journal entry that Cady had written yesterday evening. If the motion sensors would detect something, he would be notified immediately.

June 13th, 2010

The most amazing thing happened tonight. James Sullivan, the guy that I almost dated at one time came to my house drunk. I could not believe that this guy still had the hotts for me. He was outside my window and asked me to go outside. When I did, and confronted him about leaving me alone he tried to hit me, I couldn't believe it. This guy didn't seem like the type to hit a girl, but I guess alcohol does that to people. Anyway, when he tried to hit me, Gabriel stopped him. It's as if he appeared out of nowhere to save me. I was so shaken up at first, but couldn't believe that Gabriel had beaten this guy so badly that he could barely stand up on his own. I am not a fan of violence, but we live in a violent world. I wanted to thank Gabriel better than acting like a scared little girl but I couldn't muster up the courage. Tomorrow I am going to ask him again to show me how to defend myself should the situation arise.

I would love to ask Gabriel out, but I am such an old fashioned girl and a coward. I haven't dated in awhile; I wouldn't even know where to begin. I hope he has feelings for me, but I can't tell. Usually I can read people's intentions better than that but Gabriel is like a blank slate.

Gabriel could not believe what he was reading. He knew that flirting with a female target was all part of the job but it was different with Cady. *I guess I kind of like her too,* he thought. Gabriel shook off the feeling and continued reading.

Gabriel is much more that he says he is. I don't know what he knows, who he is, or how he came to be here but I am grateful. Even if it turns out that he isn't interested in me, I am happy to have met him. He is such an enigma; kind, gentle, funny, smart and let's not forget really good looking. Should I say gentle? Well he is gentle towards me; it's as if he only wants to protect me. Maybe I am delusional, but I really hope that I can go on a date with him and get to know the real Gabriel.

Gabriel was dumbfounded at what he had just read. There to protect her? He suddenly felt extreme guilt at the real reason he was in this small town. Thinking back to all of his other jobs, Gabriel could think of no time when he felt the least bit of guilt for what he had done. This job was completely different. It's as if Cady believes he is her guardian angel but nothing could be farther from the truth.

Gabriel wanted to read more of her writings from past dates to get more of a feel for her mentality, but decided against it. It was time to focus on the job at hand. As soon as he got the green light from Marcus he would have to kill her, quick and clean. *I wish there was a way out of this for her,* he thought. *This situation is just too serious for a girl who....* Gabriel's train of thought was lost when his laptop turned deep red and sounded an alarm. The motion alarm in the Bishop's house was going crazy. Gabriel looked into the monitors and saw a dark figure emerge from upstairs closet. *He must have been waiting in there for Cady to return and decided that a better hiding spot was in order.* The man moved into Cady's room and looked for a new place to hide until her return. Gabriel thought for a minute of just leaving the man to his devices and clearing out; the job would be done without him. Deciding that Cady deserved better than some private contracted asshole with a knife and piano wire, he quickly raised his rifle from the window and looked through the scope. *The very least she deserves is a quick death, one that I can deliver, not some idiot who likes it slow and messy.*

Taking aim through Cady's open window, Gabriel saw the figure walk over to her bed and pick up a stuffed teddy bear that she slept beside. The man, standing 6'2" looked to weight around 180 had a grisly beard and a tattoo on his right arm of a swastika. *Ignorant bastard,* Gabriel thought. Attached to the man's hip was a large hunting knife as Gabriel had suspected. Gabriel took a snapshot of the man through his photographic scope and uploaded it into his computer. He quickly ran the man's face through known assassins operating today. The results came back quickly and Gabriel was appalled at the man's resume. Franklin Herbert Granger was a low level assassin with a list of kills a mile long. Looking at the grizzly crime scene photos attached to his file, Gabriel noticed that everyone this man had killed was brutal and slow.

Raising his rifle again he found the man standing over Cady's desk, looking through her laptop, he decided it was time to end it. Taking sight of the man's head through the scope, Gabriel began to slowly squeeze the trigger. As Gabriel's finger neared the firing point of the trigger, the man looked up, almost as if he were looking at Gabriel from across the street, but it was too late to act. Gabriel had fired a shot before the man could react. A spurt of blood sprang from Grangers head and it was over. Placing his rifle on the ground and grabbing his silenced 9mm Beretta from the table, Gabriel quickly moved out of the apartment and across the street. Entering through the front door, Gabriel bounded up the stairs and into Cady's room. Finding the man on the floor in the same place he had fallen. Gabriel raised his weapon and pointed it at the man. Approaching quickly, Gabriel brushed the knife that had fallen from Granger's belt out of the way. He saw that the man had moved slightly when the shot was fired, catching him in the neck. Granger lay on the floor trying to get a breath but could not due to the blood pooling around his neck. Gabriel's shot had severed his windpipe, a fatal shot, but by no means meant immediate death. The man looked up at Gabriel in horror, eyes widening.

"I was just doing my job," choked Granger.

"So am I," retorted Gabriel raising his weapon and firing two shots into Granger's forehead.

"So am I," he said again.

Chapter 11
Abandonment Issues

Cady sat with her father at the Americno Café. Always finding reason to divert his attention, Martin Bishop was on the phone with this new assistant Eva. Cady, like any girl in her situation resented her father or never paying attention to her. Besides Christmas, her father was either at their office in Los Angeles, or out of state on business. Reading the menu, Cady felt abandoned as usual with her father turning his attention to his business. Cady was famished and her father was not helping matters. Every time the waitress came around he would put his finger up as if to say "one minute."

This time Cady did not care if her father was ready or not, she saw the waitress coming and decided it was time to order. The waitress approached with a smile on her face as she had done three times before. Cady could sense that the poor waitress was growing impatient with her father.

"Are you folks ready to order," asked the waitress.

Martin raised his finger again but before the waitress could look displeased Cady reached out and stopped her.

"I'm ready, and I don't care if he ever orders."

The waitress took Cady's order and turned her attention back to Martin Bishop. Now off the phone, obviously sensing the animosity he had created between him and Cady.

"Honey, what's wrong," asked her father.

"I would like to spend one evening or at the very least, one meal with my father."

"I'm sorry honey; we have been swamped with bringing the plant into a mass production phase to match Techmill. These guys are really destroying our bottom line."

"Did it ever occur to you that I don't care about your bottom line, I just want my father," Cady fumed.

Martin had obviously gotten the message and reached down to turn off his phone. When the food arrived, they sat and ate quietly. Cady ordered a scoop of chocolate ice cream for dessert and her father to her surprise ordered a chocolate milkshake.

"Wow dad, I'm surprised that you actually ordered desert. Usually you just sit and watch me eat."

"Life is too short to watch people do anything anymore, I do want to share at least a few things with my daughter," he said cracking a smile. "So your new boyfriend seems nice. It's not every day that someone formally introduces themselves to a girl's father."

"He' not my boyfriend dad, just a really great guy that moved in across the street and actually saved me from a wicked beating the other night."

"What," Martin asked disturbed.

Cady began recounting the drunken fight that James had started and told him everything from the time Gabriel stopped him from hitting her, to the sheriff taking James away. Her father looked appalled at what she was telling him. Cady could see that what she had said really bothered him; it's not every day that his mouth hung open as he listened on her every word.

"So this boy James is in jail now?"

"No," Cady said. "The sheriff drove him home to sleep it off, Gabe and I told him that we wouldn't press charges."

"Won't press charges? I'll press charges. Cady, this boy tried to hurt you; he needs to learn a lesson."

"I think Gabe taught him a pretty good lesson, James could barely walk after he had finished with him."

"It seems I owe this boy a debt of gratitude," said Martin.

"Just leave him alone, he doesn't need someone bringing up bad events from the other night. Especially when it might hurt my chances with him," she said under her breath.

"All right honey he seems like a good boy, just be careful out there, you never know who would want to hurt you."

"Gabriel wouldn't hurt me, if he wanted to he could have left James beat me up."

"It seems that way, but be careful none-the-less."

Chapter 12
Messy

Cleaning up a body was never an easy task. It was nice when one had the proper cleaning tools, such as a body bag and blood cleaner. Gabriel had finished mopping up the floor of Cady's bedroom and was now preparing to wipe down the walls. Reaching down to his vibrating cell phone, he looked at the caller ID and saw ALEX. Placing the cleaning materials on the floor, he flipped open his phone.

"What's up," asked Gabriel.

"The Bishops are on their way home," answered Alex.

"Great, the one-time this girl doesn't stay out and I'm stuck cleaning a body in her room."

"What," Alex yelled with a start.

"Freelancer stopped by for a visit. I showed him that he was not welcome in their home."

"How much time do you need," Alex asked.

"Not much, maybe ten minutes. I just have to wipe off the walls and get the body out of here."

"We're ok then, they are twenty minutes out. I'll be there as soon as I can to help with the body."

Gabriel clicked his phone shut and continued with the cleaning. *Thank god she has latex paint or this blood would never come out,* he thought. Taking nearly fifteen minutes to clean the wall was unexpected, but this assassin did spill a good deal of blood. Finishing with the walls and grabbing the body, he slowly heaved the dead assassin up onto his shoulder and left Cady's room. Walking down the stairs, Gabriel saw a Cady's red Mustang pull into the driveway. *I hate being rushed,* he thought as he took the body out the back door. Just as Gabriel closed the back door, Cady and her father walked into the front foyer.

Gabriel hurried through the yard and onto the street hoping that Cady or her father did not spot him. *It may be a little detrimental for Cady to see me carrying a dead body,* he thought to himself. Walking behind the apartment complex and tossing the body of the dead assassin onto the ground, he spotted Alex in standing near the dumpster. Walking toward Gabriel with a smile, Alex looked as if he had some quip about what had transpired, and Gabriel wasn't disappointed.

"Can't leave you alone for a minute," joked Alex.

"Why did I get the sense you would say something like that," retorted Gabriel.

"Who was he," Alex asked pointing to the corpse.

"Franklin Herbert Granger, Age forty one, low level freelancer. He was going to take our target with a hunting knife," Gabriel Answered.

"Well, I guess this is bad news," said Alex.

"Yep, whoever hired the Choir to kill Cady also put her on the open market."

"So one question partner, I know you're on the fence about completing this job, so why didn't you let Granger take the kill?"

"She's an innocent," said Gabriel. "She deserves much better than a man hiding in her closet with a large knife."

Alex didn't say another word, he just moved to the body and helped Gabriel lift him into their black Ford Escape SUV that the Choir had issued them for the job. They heaved the body into the back hatch of the vehicle and Gabriel moved for the driver's seat. Opening the door and climbing inside, Gabriel could tell that Alex was disappointed that the job was not over yet. *I'm just not ready to kill her,* he thought.

"Do we have a problem," Gabriel asked.

"It would have been nice to be on our way out of this little town by now."

"Alex, the job will be done and we will be out of here by the end of the week," Gabriel said, sounding disappointed.

"You're having second thoughts about this job aren't you?"

Gabriel lowered his head and started the vehicle. Looking back at Alex without saying a word, he then turned his attention to the road as they pulled out of the drive. Gabriel didn't need to say anything; Alex could tell that he didn't want to kill the girl. He had always known that Gabriel was against killing an innocent, but if they didn't, Marcus would consider them AWOL and send someone to kill the girl anyway, then whomever he sent, would come for the boys too.

Twenty minutes later they pulled onto a small forest path in the town of Smithly and crawled out of the car. It had been a very quiet ride for them, and Gabriel had to wonder if he didn't complete the job, if Alex would. The Choir acts more like the Italian Mafia in that respect. If you slip up, it's not a stranger they send for you, it's usually someone you know and trust; it could even be your best friend.

Pulling the body out of the car and unzipping the body bag, Gabriel grabbed Granger's body by the feet and Alex took the head. They walked back into the forest for nearly ten minutes before finding a suitable place to dump the body.

"Perfect," Gabriel said, looking at an old drainage pipe they had come across.

Alex removed the grating while Gabriel slid Granger's body inside. *It doesn't matter if anyone finds the body; we just have to hide it long enough to get the job done and get out of town,* thought Gabriel.

Alex placed the grate back over the drainage pipe and moved closer to Gabriel. It was difficult for Gabriel to look at his partner but when he managed Alex stood with an uneasy smile on his face.

"Gabe, if you don't want to do this job then don't, let me take point and I'll complete the mission."

"As flattering as your proposal is, I think I'll handle it just the same," said Gabriel trying to look strong.

"You got it, but get your shit together, Marcus will be giving us the green light any day now," reported Alex.

Gabriel knew that Alex was right. Marcus would be in contact soon to give them the green light on Cady's murder. In their line of work, things change almost hourly. One minute they could be on a surveillance mission and the next ordered to take them out. Of course, the opposite was also true. They might be here to kill someone and the job would be cancelled before it was completed. Gabriel truly hoped that this job would be one of those instances.

Chapter 13
Looking For An Out

Gabriel and Alex walked back into the apartment still hardly speaking to each other. Alex decided to take the first watch, sitting in the recliner and pulling a rifle scope from his bag on the floor. Looking through Cady's window he saw her getting ready for bed. Wearing what appeared to be a white silk night shirt, she sat brushing her hair. Alex kept his attention on Cady but occasionally looked at the monitor on his laptop to see what Mr. Bishop was up to. Martin appeared to already be in bed with the covers pulled all the way up to his neck. Alex turned his attention back to Cady who had now flipped on the television in her room and began watching a show that Alex himself loved, Family Guy.

Gabriel sat at his computer and began typing his report for the day when a connection notice flashed onto his screen. Before he could hit the accept button, it was apparently overridden and a very disgruntled Marcus appeared on the monitor.

"Report."

Gabriel looked surprised at Marcus's face, he never appeared mad to him before. Gabriel shrugged it off and recounted the day' events.

"Martin Bishop has returned home, he and the target went out for dinner and were followed by Alexander. Nothing substantial to report on their conversation. I had a run in with a freelancer who was apparently green lighted for the kill."

"I take it that the girl is still alive and Granger is dead," asked Marcus.

Gabriel was in total shock at what Marcus had just said. *He knows who came for Cady? How in the hell could he know that?*

"Marcus, how do you know the freelancers name?"

"I contracted him outside of the Agency; I wanted this mess to end before it had gotten out of hand."

"Out of hand," said Gabriel outraged. "Now it's out of hand, I almost didn't get the place cleaned up before the Bishops returned home. Marcus, how dare you undermine me on this job!"

"Gabriel it was not my intention to undermine you. I want this job done as quickly as you do. I also know that you are conflicted about completing this job. I don't want to lose one of my best, so I sent a freelancer to complete the kill."

"Conflicted, hell yes I'm conflicted, she's an innocent. She didn't do anything to deserve this. If you want the father dead, then fine, but the girl should remain unharmed."

"That is not the contract Gabriel, and if you won't complete the contract, then we can deal with that later, but let me know now if you are refusing this job."

"No sir," retorted Gabriel. "I will complete the mission. I take it then that the girl has been green lighted through the Choir then?"

"As of this moment, you have authorization to make the kill."

"Good, it will be done tomorrow," muttered Gabriel.

"Yes it will; I made sure of that."

"What are you talking about," asked Gabriel.

"I've sent another to make sure this job ends tomorrow. Raphael will be joining you tomorrow evening for the kill to make sure there are no mistakes. He should arrive sometime around eleven p.m."

"I told you I have it under control Marcus, I will complete the job tomorrow."

"And if you do, Gabriel, then there will be no repercussions, but if you fail, Raphael will make sure to tie up any loose ends," said Marcus before disappearing from the screen.

Gabriel put his head in his hands and closed his eyes. He knew that if he refused to kill Cady tomorrow, then Raphael would, then turn his sights on the both of them. *Focus idiot, you have this under control. You just need to kill the girl tomorrow and all will be well.* Gabriel rose from the chair and moved to where Alex sat watching Cady.

Placing a hand on Alex's shoulder, he knew that his partner had reported a problem to Marcus, even if he did mean to help Gabriel.

"We have a green light for tomorrow night," said Gabriel.

"Good, this mess ends tomorrow."

"One way or another," said Gabriel.

"What do you mean by that?"

"Marcus has sent Raphael; he will be in around eleven tomorrow night. He said if I kill her then we will be fine, but if Raphael has to do it, then he will mop us up too."

"Damn," said Alex.

"What are we going to do Gabe? I know you don't want to do this, and I don't either but what choice do we have?"

"Like I said Alex, it ends tomorrow, one way or another."

Gabriel went back to his laptop and continued typing his report. *Alex is conflicted too, I can tell,* he thought. Gabriel had to admit to himself that he had thought about not killing the girl, but this was just too heavy, and she was too important to the Choir not to terminate. *What a mess,* he thought again. *Pull yourself together, this job needs to be completed tomorrow, and I have to do it. I don't care about myself, but Alex is counting on me not to get him killed.*

Pulling his silenced Beretta pistol from his waistband, he began taking it apart and cleaning it for tomorrow. Everything has to be perfect. *I don't want her to suffer and the only thing I can offer is a quick and painless death.*

Chapter 14
Asking Him Out

Cady awoke with a start. Sitting straight up in bed, she looked out her window and saw daylight streaming through. She hated bad dreams, especially when it was about the guy she thought was her protector. Closing her eyes trying to remember the whole dream, she saw Gabriel standing in her room with a gun pointing at her. Smiling, and without saying a word, he emptied the gun into her body.

Unfortunately, that was all she could remember. Cady had many bad dreams, most of them about her father, but this one was different and it seemed so real. She slowly rose from bed and walked down the hall to get a shower. Turning on the hot water, and letting it run for a while, she slipped off her clothes and stepped in. Cady wanted to look her best tonight. She was going to ask Gabriel out on a date, on the anniversary of his parent's death and show him that this day couldn't be all bad. It was a Friday, so she determined her father would have no problem letting her stay out late, she was nineteen after all.

When she finished with her shower, she tied her hair up in a pony tail and put on a pair of jeans and a white t-shirt, which she suspected made her look more like a guy. She thought that if Gabriel just thought about getting out and having some fun it would be easier if she looked like one of the guys when she asked him out. Not exactly a fool proof plan, but it had to work. Later, before the date, she would put on her makeup, do her hair and put on a nice dress.

Looking out her bedroom window, she could see that Gabriel was not outside, so she decided to go over to his apartment. Practically running down the stairs and out the door, she slowed herself to a walk before anyone could see how excited she was, especially Gabriel. Making her way to the apartment building across the street, she opened the door and began walking up the stairs. Apparently Gabriel had known she was coming over because when she reached the second landing he was descending toward her.

Gabriel looked grief stricken and Cady could tell that it was probably due to his parents being killed in a car accident last year. When Gabriel had reached the second landing without saying a word, Cady began having second thoughts about asking him out. *No guts, no glory girl, it's now or never,* she thought to herself.

"Hi Gabe"

"Hi," was all he said in return.

"Want to go for a walk?"

"I would like that," he said breaking a small smile.

Cady and Gabriel left the apartment and started walking down the street. Gabriel still looked distraught and Cady knew that something had to be done.

"So Gabe, you want to go out tonight?"

Cady was shocked that she had just blurted that out, but was also kind of proud of herself. Gabriel was staring at the ground and slowed his pace. Looking up at Cady with his bright green eyes, the eyes she also had, but loved on his strong face.

"I don't think so Cady, maybe some other time."

Cady knew he might say something like that and had her protest already waiting.

"I still owe you for saving me from getting beat up, and for teaching me some moves. I'm not taking no for an answer Gabe. I have promised myself that I was taking you out tonight, so don't make me a promise breaker."

Gabriel was still looking at her, almost longingly. She had hoped that he would just come out and say yes, but she knew that she would probably have to work harder.

"I would love to, really, but I have some work to do tonight," he responded.

"Well what time do you have to work?"

"Eleven."

"Well Gabe, I'll make you a promise; I promise to have you home by eleven, and if you are still uncomfortable with going out with me, then I promise not to rape you," she said with a sly smile.

Gabriel started laughing, something Cady was hoping to see. She absolutely loved his smile, and hardly ever got to see it since she had met him last week.

"All right, if you have me back by eleven, then I'll go out with you."

Cady was ecstatic, but tried not to show it. She could not help but give him a big smile however. As they continued their walk down the street, they didn't say much, but continued to smile at one another. Gabriel was the first to break the uncomfortable silence.

"So where are you whisking me away to?"

"Well I was thinking of a place called Dave and Busters."

"What is that," Gabriel asked.

"It's a lot of fun, you go in and eat and then you can go back and play a bunch of videogames."

"Sounds like fun, what should I wear?"

"Anything you want, see what I have on? It's a pretty relaxed place."

Gabriel smiled at her again, obviously more comfortable with the date than he had been. She hoped that tonight he would want to continue going out with her after tonight, but decided to take it one step at a time.

When they had rounded the next corner, Cady realized that they were already home. *Time flies when you're trying to get a date,* she thought. Gabriel had walked with her all the way to her door, and had stared at her oddly.

"What's up Gabe," she asked.

"Nothing, it will be good to get my mind off of things, even for a while. Thanks Cady."

"Any time, but I have to go inside and tell my dad where I am going tonight or he will have the National Guard looking for me by eight."

"Alright," Gabriel said laughing again.

"See you around 5," she asked.

"I'll be here."

Cady opened the door and stepped inside, smiling at Gabriel, she closed the door. Once the door latched shut, she began dancing and jumping with excitement. It would have been a nice little dance if her father would not have entered the hallway to see what the ruckus was and saw what she was doing.

"You really like him don't you honey," Martin Bishop said.

Cady stopped dancing and looked embarrassingly at her father.

"Yea, I really do," she said.

"From the dance you are doing, I suspect you two have plans tonight."

"We are going out, but he has to do some kind of work at eleven, so I'll be home around then."

"Alright honey, but be careful out there."

"You always say that and nothing ever happens dad, you're too paranoid."

Martin bishop walked into his study after a short conversation with his daughter. *Cady is going out with a boy tonight. I still remember my little baby in diapers.* Turning on his computer he quickly checked the files on a new development his R&D Division had on a new computer chip. While Martin browsed the new findings on the chip a call came in on his business line. Reaching to answer the phone, Martin checked the Caller ID. The call was coming from his office in Los Angeles.

"This is Bishop."

"Mr. Bishop, its Derek Moore in Special Projects."

"Yes Derek, do you have any news?"

"I'm afraid so sir. It turns out that General Tanaka had connection with the Chinese Triads. He did indeed contract a hit on your daughter."

"Do we know when it's coming?"

"The information is sketchy, but I have a source from NTT News. I'm meeting him tonight because he wouldn't talk over the phone," said Derek.

"Do we currently know anything," asked Bishop.

"We have some leads but nothing solid, except…" Derek trailed off.

"Except what," Bishop demanded.

"Well sir, it seems that the organization called The Choir was the one that got the contract on your daughter. These guys mean business; supposedly they are the best in the world."

"Keep me posted, I don't care what time it is, I want to know what your source tells you," Bishop said as he clicked the disconnect button on the phone.

Chapter 15
First Date

Gabriel sat on his bed in a bath towel. He thought a hot shower would steady his nerves but it didn't. He was still looking for a way out of this contract but saw no other option but to end the girl's life. Gabriel stood up and looked at the clock which read 4:29. He moved to his closet and put on a pair of jeans and a black t-shirt. Picking up his gun from the nightstand and tucking it away in his back waistband, he slid on his black leather jacket and moved for the door where Alex was waiting with his keys.

"You set," asked Alex.

"Yea, I'm going to complete the job before Raphael gets here."

"Alright, but I want you to understand something before you do this." Alex paused for a long second before continuing. "Whatever happens tonight, I want you to know that I stand beside your decision, whatever that may be."

Gabriel smiled and nodded to Alex as he pulled open the door and closed it quickly behind him. He raced down the stairs and out the back door of the apartment building. Looking at his watch as he hurried toward the SUV it now read 4:55. Climbing into the vehicle and making the engine roar to life, he pulled out and circled the block before stopping at the Bishop residence.

Stepping out of the SUV and slowly making his way to the front door, Gabriel thought about all of his jobs in the past, and how he had never actually been on a date. He guessed that finding the time was the major culprit in that, but shook off the thoughts and assured himself, *this is only a job, not a date*. When he reached the front door Martin Bishop met him before he could ring the bell.

"Change of plans son, Cady needs to stay home tonight."

"DAD," called Cady from the top of the stairs.

Gabriel could not see Cady but knew that the argument may take a while. Martin Bishop closed the door before Gabriel could see what had transpired. He stood outside listening to the heated conversation that Bishop and his daughter were having.

"I'm not a little kid anymore; you can't keep doing this to me."

"Honey, I'm just trying to protect you," he heard Bishop retort.

"Protect me from what, a normal life? I'm nineteen years old and I AM going out with Gabriel tonight."

Gabriel heard some muffled tones trailing off deeper into the house before the door opened again. Gabriel saw Cady standing in the doorway wearing a black dress down to her knees, diamond earrings, and her hair was scrunched and wavy.

"Wow, you look really beautiful," Gabriel choked.

"Thanks Gabe, I'm told I clean up well."

"You never looked dirty," Gabriel said with a smile.

"I'm glad for that," Cady laughed.

"I thought we would take my car tonight, if that's ok."

"Great," Cady said as she began walking.

As they drove off Gabriel could see Martin Bishop standing in the doorway of the house. He honked the horn and pulled out. Gabriel was clear on his objective tonight, but it did make him uncomfortable that Cady and her father were in an argument and it would be the last time she spoke to him.

"So Dave and Busters huh," said Gabriel.

"You will have a blast Gabe, its right up your alley."

Gabriel shot a quick smile to Cady and continued driving. Thinking about what must be done after dinner really wound him up. It was as if Marcus had sent him here to test his resolve. *What the hell do I still have to prove to Marcus and what did Alex mean when he said; whatever happens tonight.* Gabriel thought of all possible meanings to the statement and it was as if Alex was asking him not to go through with this. It was very interesting since Alex had reported Gabriel's faltering loyalty just a day ago. Gabriel tried to take his mind off of things by striking up a conversation with Cady.

"So even though we have to be back by eleven, we will still have some time after dinner, what do you want to do?"

"I picked dinner," she said. "The rest is up to you."

Gabriel already had a plan for after dinner, but Cady wouldn't like it. He had thought about the time and place to kill her all day long. He would pull onto the overlook, a small cliff at the edge of town, shoot her in the head, and leave her body. Not the most artistic kill that Gabriel had preformed, but Cady deserved a straight forward kill, and Gabriel really had no desire to make this kill high profile.

Gabriel could feel the cold steel of his gun pressing into his lower back. At times, he actually liked the feeling, but not tonight. He thought he might cry when she died, but Gabriel had to hold strong, *who knows who may be watching,* he thought. Pulling into the restaurant Gabriel found a parking space right up front and they both exited the car and walked inside.

Gabriel and Cady were seated immediately and ordered an appetizer. Cady could tell the something was truly wrong with Gabriel. Guessing that he was still broken up over his parents, she decided to ask him about it.

"Gabe, what's wrong?"

"Nothing," Gabriel retorted quickly.

"Are you still in mourning your parent's death?"

Gabriel looked distraught. Cady had no idea who he really was, or what he was there for.

"I'm in morning, yes, but not for my parents," he admitted.

"Then for who," Cady asked.

Gabriel then put on a fake smile for Cady and tried to look like he was having a good time.

"Never mind, I just want to focus on having a good time with you tonight," said Gabriel.

Cady smiled back. She was happy that Gabriel was looking forward to spending time with her. *He is something truly special,* she thought.

"You know Gabe, I am really happy that I met you."

You won't be happy that you met me in a few hours, he thought.

"I'm glad I met you too Cady, you have really made me reevaluate what is important in life."

Cady smiled another big smile. She knew she was gaining ground with him and hoped that soon he would let her in. The problem was, as Gabriel knew, is that she had already been let in, and it was tearing him apart.

Their appetizer arrived and by the time they had finished it and their entrée's came; Gabriel was truly having a good time. Laughing with Cady was intoxicating. He had certainly never met anyone like her, and knew that she was one of a kind. After dinner, they decided to play some games in the back room. Cady led him into what looked like a Vegas casino, but was full of video games and prizes.

Gabriel decided that he would win her a prize, to give her a great feeling before she died. Walking over to the ski ball area, he plugged in some quarters and tossed the ball but never really hit the high point rings. Cady stood and laughed as he frustrated himself and lost the game. The machine, as if it were ridiculing him, spit out one ticket.

"One ticket, 10,000 more to go," Cady said laughing.

Cady led Gabriel to a shooting game called "Time Crisis 4" and they both plugged in some quarters to play together. When the game started, Gabriel began shooting all of the bad guys in the room. Every time Cady drew her gun and pointed it at someone they were already dead. Amazed at how accurate Gabriel was at the game she handed him her pistol and he took off on a rampage. Killing everything on the screen, the machine was spitting out tickets like it was New Year's confetti.

When the onslaught was over, Cady had looked down and saw the mountain of tickets on the floor. Looking back at the screen, Gabriel was watching the final bit of storyline in the game. She was amazed that he had beaten this game with only fifty cents. She had never seen someone play this game so accurately. Gabriel turned around when the credits started rolling and saw Cady's green eyes staring in amazement.

"Alex and I have always been pretty good at shooters," he said.

"You must practice eight hours a day," she responded.

"Sometimes more," Gabriel said smiling.

The couple moved to a room that was full of prizes. Gabriel handed the attendant the pile of tickets and the man notified them that they had 60,001 tickets to redeem which was the jackpot on Time Crisis combined with his one pathetic ticket from ski ball. Cady looked around at some of the odds and ends that they had in the prize room and Gabriel followed closely behind her.

"Pick whatever you want, I was trying to win you a prize," said Gabriel.

Cady smiled again and walked through the store and found a large stuffed bear with angel wings and a halo. She picked it up and showed Gabriel.

"It's perfect," she said taking the bear to the attendant.

Once the attendant had cashed out their tickets and given Cady back the bear, Cady turned to Gabriel and giggled.

"What are you laughing at," asked Gabriel.

"You like him," Cady asked showing him the stuffed animal.

"If you like him, I like him," he said.

"Good, because I named him Gabriel, he's my guardian angel."

Gabriel smiled and held Cady's hand as they walked to the exit. *There it is again, she is calling me her guardian angel,* he thought.

Chapter 16
The Angel of Mercy

Gabriel and Cady had left the restaurant and were now on their way to their final destination together. Gabriel had had a really great time with Cady tonight and now regretted even more what he must do. When they neared the overlook Cady began looking inquisitive.

"I thought you had to be back by eleven," she said.

"I do, but it's only ten, and I'm not ready for this night to end just yet."

They pulled into the middle of the overlook and stared over the dash at the shining lights of the small town. Cady stepped out of the SUV for a closer look and Gabriel followed, exiting the driver side. They pulled themselves onto the hood of the SUV and lay with their heads resting on the windshield. Cady, knowing the area was completely deserted except for her and Gabriel began looking at the stars in wonder.

"Gabe, do you think there is such thing as fate?"

"I truly hope not," said Gabriel.

"What makes you say that?"

Gabriel looked uncomfortable for a minute, trying to choose the right words for his view on such a topic. Slowly turning his head to Cady, he breathed a small sigh.

"I believe that there is a path leading to certain choices in life, and every choice is a fork in the road. We get to make the choice based on who we are at the time. I also believe that every road leads to a different ending whether it is happy or sad. So fate does exist in some form, but we get to decide our futures, not some pre-written destiny.

Cady looked amazed at the answer, smiling at Gabriel, she knew that he was much smarter than he led her to believe.

"That's amazing; I see you have thought about the question before."

"Only recently," said Gabriel.

The couple sat looking up at the stars for a few more moments, and enjoyed each other's company. Gabriel still could not figure out what was happening to his body when he was close to Cady. His finger tingled, knees felt as if they would buckle, and his heart ached because of what he knew must be done.

Standing on the edge of the cliff, Cady appeared to be as happy as Gabriel had ever seen her. Standing beside her, he knew it was time. Before he could pull his gun from behind him Cady turned to him with another smile on her face.

"Gabriel, I'm not sure how to tell you this," she began.

"What is it Cady, you know you can tell me anything."

"Well, since I met you, I have been really happy. My father is always gone, and Jan is really my only friend. You changed all that. Gabe, I really like you, and I hope that we can continue to see each other. I don't mean as friends either, I have wanted to be near you ever since I met you in my yard the first day you came over."

"So you want me to be your boyfriend," Gabriel asked taken aback.

"Yea," Cady said with an embarrassed smile.

"Cady, there is a great deal of complications in my life, and I doubt that you would ever want to be a part of that. I'm really not who you think I am."

"You are exactly who I think you are Gabe. You are an amazing person; kind, gentle, funny, and really smart. Isn't that what matters? I would be willing to help you with anything that comes along, I want to be there."

Gabriel had his right hand behind his back, holding his gun. *It's time to get this over with*, he thought. Looking deep into Cady's eyes, he closed in on her. Pulling her close with his left hand, she placed her head on his shoulder. Looking up suddenly with a bright smile, she closed the gap between them and gently placed her lips on his. Gabriel was surprised at first, but began to close his eyes and enjoy the closeness of their two bodies. Gabriel's hand fell from his gun and embraced Cady tighter. Their lips parted only for a second, in which time their foreheads touched, they stared deep into each other's eyes, smiled big smiles, and began kissing again.

For the first time, Gabriel knew what was truly important in life. It wasn't ridding the world of corruption; it wasn't the killing of violent criminals that would most certainly hurt others if given the chance; it was right here, right now. Being in the arms of another; caring for them more than caring for one's self. Gabriel knew in this moment, that he was in love.

Chapter 17
Assassin's Plural

Martin Bishop waited by the phone in his study. Any minute he would be receiving a call from Derek Moore about the assassin that had come for his daughter. He had been spending a huge chunk of his time ensuring the protection of his daughter, and tonight he might just get the break he was looking for. Bishop had devoted his special projects division to finding any information on the killer and when he would be coming for his daughter. He knew that General Tanaka would not send him right away; he would wait until Martin felt comfortable and safe, that nothing would happen to his daughter, and then he would strike. Unfortunately, General Tanaka had no idea that Martin Bishop would never feel safe again.

The phone suddenly sounded and Martin picked up the receiver before it could finish its first ring.

"This is Bishop, what have you got?"

"Not much sir, but it's a break."

"Derek, tell me everything you know immediately."

"Well sir, like I said, there is not much to go on but I do have a clue to their identity."

"What do you have, a name, photograph, what? I need this assassin to be in the ground before he reaches my daughter."

"Not assassin Mr. Bishop, assassin's. My source from NTT tells me that there are two of them coming for her. My source also tells me that their identity's never change. They will be named after Angels."

"Angels," said Martin. "I'm not familiar with the names of the angels. I know there was a Michael the archangel."

"They don't have to be mentioned specifically in the Bible, any historical text will do. I have some names, but keep in mind; it may not be the names we are looking for."

"Go ahead, I'll write them down," said Martin as he pulled out a notepad and pen."

"Ok, well there is the one you know about Michael. He is supposedly the very best of the Choir, but my source says that he is out of the country." The rest are Uriel, Jeremiel, Raphael, Alexander, and Gabriel."

Martin Bishop's heart stopped when he heard Gabriel's name. He thought about the young boy, *Could he really be an assassin.* Martin got himself under control and continued writing. As he neared the end of names that Derek had rattled off, he tried to think back to Gabriel. *What was the name of his brother that moved out here with him...Alex, he thought.*

"Derek, you said that these men don't change their names, but do they ever shorten them? Such as Alexander as..."

"Alex," Derek broke in, yes, my source tells me that an assassin named Alex has been recorded in some of the kills he had reported on. Also, we have a photo of three assassins known to be working for the Choir now. I'm uploading them to your compute as we speak."

Martin turned his attention to the monitor and saw the first picture flash up. The first was a female with blond hair and blue eyes.

"Haven't seen this one around," reported Martin.

"Her name is Arial," said Derek. "Next we have a man named Azrael."

The picture of a man flashed onto the screen with brown hair and brown eyes. This man looked like the typical assassin, disgruntled and dangerous.

"Nothing David, what else have you got."

"I have a security camera still of the one they call Gabriel. It' grainy, but this is the first and only time that this guy slipped up and let himself be photographed. Apparently, the FBI is actively looking for him in connection with the Death of Senator O'Malley two years ago."

The picture flashed up on the screen and Martin stared in horror as the man's bright green eyes stared back at him. Grief stricken, Martin had realized what was now happening.

"Martin, are you ok," asked David.

"David, I need you to mobilize my private security now."

"Sir, I was informed that the assassins wouldn't even be in town for another month."

"Your source was wrong," said Martin gasping for breath.

"Sir, are you all right, I trust my source."

"Your source lied to you David, the assassin's are already here, and my daughter is with one of them right now."

Chapter 18
Raphael

Pulling into Cady's driveway, Gabriel placed the car in park and turned to Cady to see her smiling at him as she had been doing all night. Looking down at the clock on the dash, it read 11:40.

"You're late for work," said Cady.

"Yea, well, I still have to go to work tonight, but only to hand in my resignation."

Gabriel and Cady stepped out of the SUV and he walked her to the door. Turning for another kiss, Cady leaned in and embraced Gabriel once more. It was Cady who broke the kiss but did not pull away from Gabriel. Cady stood on up onto her toes and whispered to Gabriel.

"How long can this last? I know it's childish to say such a thing, only knowing you for a week, but it feels so right. I want to be with you forever."

"Forever it is then," Gabriel whispered back.

Cady finally pulled away from Gabriel and stood with the largest smile he had seen on Cady since he had met her. Cady opened the door and stepped inside. Smiling one more smile before she closed the door, Gabriel watched until it closed and latched before turning and walking back to his SUV. Before stepping into the vehicle, he could hear Cady and her father in another argument, which sounded as if it were coming from her bedroom. Gabriel decided not to try to listen in; he had other fish to fry. Raphael would be in town and he needed to be reasoned with.

When Gabriel got back to the apartment, he found Alex in nearly the same place he had left him.

"You turned off your phone," said a distressed looking Alex.

"Yea, I wanted peace and quiet tonight."

Gabriel looked around and found their bags were packed and waiting at the front door. He looked at Alex puzzled and saw the look of worry on his face.

"What's wrong," asked Gabriel.

"Bishop knows who we are, we are exposed."

"What," screamed Gabriel running to his laptop and turning on the monitors to see what was happening in the Bishop house, but found only a blank screen. Puzzled, Gabriel looked back to Alex.

"He found our cameras, and our listening devices. He has also called in a hit squad of his own, they will be here in two hours, we have to pull out now, but at least the job is done."

"Well," Gabriel said cringing.

"She is still alive," asked Alex.

"Yes, she is still alive Alex, I couldn't do it."

Alex actually looked relieved at what Gabriel had just said.

"I was hoping that you wouldn't. I had been thinking about this job for a while, and it just doesn't sit right with me to kill an innocent."

"Same here," began Gabriel, we have to wait for Raphael; maybe we can talk him out of this."

"He should have been here by now; it's not like him to be late."

Alex moved to collect Gabriel's laptop and place it in its case. Accidentally bumping the window, he activated the heat sensor that they had been mounted there to monitor the Bishop's movements.

"Hey Gabe, take a look at this."

Gabriel walked over but did not look at the monitor, just questioningly at Alex.

"Why do you suppose I'm picking up three heat signatures in their house," Alex asked.

Gabriel's eyes widened, he knew in his heart why.

"God no," Gabriel shouted as he grabbed his weapon from his waistband and ran for the door. Alex fumbled to get his weapon from his bag to follow suit, but quickly looking through the window, he saw that Gabriel was already across the street, running at a sprint. Gabriel had no time; he launched himself into the large door of Cady's house and it fell from its hinges. Not losing a beat, he rushed up the stairs to Cady's room hoping that it was not too late. Turning right and running down the hall, he stopped at Cady's door and heard silence. Raising his weapon and kicking the bedroom door below the knob, he blew the door off of the frame and entered the room to find Raphael standing over Cady and Martin Bishop who were seated on her bed, terror stricken. Raphael turned to meet the intruder but Gabriel had the element of surprise. Gabriel fired every bullet he had in his weapon; each shot striking Raphael in the chest. The assassin fell onto the floor lifeless.

Gabriel looked at Cady who was now staring at Gabriel with an expression of horror on her face. Cady stood up from the bed and threw herself into Gabriel, laying her head below his shoulder and holding him. Her guardian angel had saved her again. Pulling Cady away from his body, he began checking her for injuries.

"Did he hurt you," asked Gabriel.

"No," she responded shaken.

Gabriel turned to Martin Bishop, who was still sitting on Cady's bed in shock staring at the dead assassin on the floor. Blood had pooled around the tall red haired man and Martin looked as if he were flashing back to his encounter in China.

"Mr. Bishop, we need to get you and your daughter out of here," said Gabriel.

Martin looked up, eyes glassed over obviously thinking that the danger had not passed yet. He slowly stood up and approached Gabriel.

"Why," asked Martin. "Why did you save us? This man was doing the same job you had set out to do."

Cady looked up suddenly with confusion on her face. Gabriel knew that she still had no idea who he really was.

"What is he talking about Gabe?"

"Cady, I told you there were complications in my life that you wouldn't be able to deal with."

Alex had now entered the bedroom and stood against the broken door frame that Gabriel had kicked in to save the Bishops. Looking at the fallen Raphael, he sighed heavily.

"Well, I guess we just retired," said Alex as a smile crossed his face.

Gabriel was not amused. He sighed heavily and realized that it was now time to tell Cady the entire story.

"Alex, help Mr. Bishop downstairs and make some coffee. We can sit down and I will explain everything," said Gabriel in a hushed tone.

Alex nodded and placed his hand on Martin's shoulder, leading him toward the stairs. Gabriel looked back at Cady and nodded for her to follow.

"I'll be right behind you."

Without saying a word, Cady crossed her arms over her chest and walked out with a sullen look. When she was out of the room, Gabriel kneeled at the side of the fallen Raphael. Turning the body onto his back, he stared into the lifeless eyes of his fellow assassin.

"I just wanted to talk about the situation. You didn't have to die tonight brother, and I'm sorry."

Gabriel reached down and ran his fingers over Raphael's face, slowly closing the assassin's eyes and putting him to his final rest. After he explained to Cady and her father the current situation, they would have to leave immediately.

Gabriel wasted no more time agonizing over his fallen brother. *I made my decision, and I have to stick this out until the end, even if Cady no longer wants to be with me,* he thought. Moving slowly down the stairs, Gabriel looked into the kitchen to find Alex making coffee and Martin Bishop who had just retrieved a blanket from the closet and placed it over his daughter's shoulders. It was time for them to know the truth.

Chapter 19
The Truth Revealed

When Gabriel entered the kitchen he could sense an air of confusion, anger and sadness. Alex had just placed coffee in front of Cady and Martin, and turned to pour himself a cup. Gabriel pulled a chair from the kitchen table and sat. Silent for a moment, Gabriel had to determine the best way to explain the situation so that everyone at the table was aware of what was happening.

Looking intently at Cady, he began to realize that she was having a hard time looking back at Gabriel. He lowered his head and began what would be, his last briefing.

"I understand that tonight has been a big shock for everyone, but I need to bring you up to speed on the current situation."

"You need to explain yourself first," Cady snapped.

"Ok, you deserve to know that too. Alex and I are both assassins working for an organization called the Choir. As you may have guessed, we lied about a great deal of information. First, Alex and I are brothers, but not by blood. Everyone working for the Choir is considered a family, and all of the assassins are brothers and sisters to us. Alex is a second class operative assigned as my partner; we have been working together for the past three years."

"Wait, second class, what does that mean," Martin asked.

"Each member of the Choir has a level of training and experience. Everyone starts at the fifth level and works their way to first class, although not many have lived to see that level."

"What class are you Gabriel; if Gabriel is your real name," Cady cut in.

Gabriel put his head down disappointed in himself for telling this many lies to Cady. *She is right to ask; she knows nothing about me.*

"Yes, my name really is Gabriel Mason. Everyone in the Choir is named after an angel or some other figure from a holy scripture. I'm almost sure that is what saved me from the same fate as my parents."

"Your parents," queried Martin.

"I was recruited into the Choir by an assassin named Michael. He was sent to kill my parents who were extorting money from a large corporation which held interest for the Choir. When Michael came for them, he completed his job quickly but since I wasn't in the contract, he spared my life and took me with him back to the Choir for training. Nearly everyone in the Choir was recruited the same way. To answer your question Cady, I am currently rated the second best assassin in the world."

"You must be so proud," she quickly retorted.

"Let's cut to the chase," said Martin. "You were sent here to kill us?"

Gabriel paused for a moment, not really knowing what to say, but decided that the truth was all he had left.

"I was only sent to kill Cady," Gabriel said softly.

Cady looked up surprised. Obviously wondering why she had been targeted.

"Why me?"

"You were chosen because of a bad deal your father made in China. I don't have the details, but apparently he pissed off a very well connected man. He took his grudge to the Triads, a well known organized crime syndicate. They contracted us to come here and kill you Cady," said Alex.

Martin Bishop stood up, and poured himself another cup of coffee. Standing with his back turned to everyone, he decided it was time to reveal what had happened on his trip to China.

"I was approached by a member of the CIA," he began. "This agent knew that we had come into possession of a new weaponized guidance chip designed for nuclear missiles. These chips enable a weapon to break off of one target and acquire a new one mid flight. The Chinese wanted these because of their interest in expanding their regime to Korea. They would launch a missile at a dummy target during a so called test, and then reprogram the missile to strike North Korea. They would have total deniability of any wrong doing, and could claim a malfunction in the guidance system."

"They could have also targeted any other country in the world claiming the same thing," chimed Alex.

"The agent wanted us to attempt a sale of these chips to a Chinese General named Tanaka. When the deal was complete, they were supposed to rush in and arrest him in a joint taskforce with the Chinese Military. During the exchange, I was shot in the lower back and my assistant Clay was killed… And so was General Tanak's son David. Later, as Tanaka was being lead away by the non-corrupt members of the Chinese Military, he promised to have any children of mine killed so that I would know his pain."

"You were shot," Cady broke in.

"He's honey, but it was minor which enabled me to come home and act as if Clay was the only one hurt in China."

"Great, Not only does my father never spend any time at home with his daughter, but he tries to get me killed too. Not to mention that both my father and my boyfriend…I mean EX boyfriend reveal that they have been lying to me."

"Honey," Martin began, but it was too late, Cady had gotten out of her hair and stormed out of the room.

"I had better go talk to her," said Martin.

"No, let me," said Gabriel.

"No offence son, but you were hired to kill us, you're the last person that she wants to talk to," interjected Martin.

"I need to speak to her in private Mr. Bishop. I understand your apprehension toward me, but I made the decision to protect your daughter from my people and I will not allow you to stop me at this point."

Martin Bishop placed his hands in his face, and ran them through his hair obviously frustrated. He nodded for Gabriel to continue after Cady. Gabriel nodded back and turned to go after the person he now treasured over anything else.

Chapter 20
Love and Hate

Sitting on the front porch swing of her house, Cady rocked back and forth trying to take in everything that Gabriel and her father had said. *My father had been in China, working for the CIA, he pissed some high ranking official off and now they want me dead,* she thought. Not noticing the door open and close, she suddenly found Gabriel standing next to her with a sympathetic look on his face. Cady could barely look at him as different feelings flowed through her body. She was well past the point of feeling sorry for herself and now she felt angry and scared at the same time. Gabriel, without saying a word sat down next to her on the swing.

"I'm sorry this had to happen to you," said Gabriel.

Cady looked disgusted as she turned to the man that she had fallen for only an hour before.

"I just don't understand any of it Gabe, what the hell is going on. One minute you and I are kissing and the next you burst through my bedroom door and shoot a man who was trying to kill us. I would consider that brave if only you weren't friends with him."

"Raphael and I were never friends, more like rivals."

"That doesn't help Gabriel."

"Sorry," he said.

Millions of things were running through her head as she sat there rocking with Gabriel, but one thing in particular stood out to her.

"You really came here to kill me," she asked silently.

"Yes," said Gabriel, lowering his head.

"So everything we have been through, dinner, friendship, and what happened on the overlook meant nothing to you?"

Gabriel raised his head and looked Cady in her beautiful green eyes. With pain on his face, the kind of pain where someone can tell that your heart if broken, he tried to tell Cady the absolute truth.

"Cady, I understand that you may not believe what I am about to tell you, but it's the truth. My boss, a man called Marcus sent Alex and I here to kill you. When I first met you, I was surprised at who you were. I have never been sent after someone that is innocent before. I was committed to doing the job, that is, until I got to know you. I started falling for you Cady, and I fell hard tonight."

Gabriel reached out to take Cady's hand, but she quickly pulled away when she felt the touch. Disappointed, Gabriel knew that he should not have tried, but wanted to feel her touch if only once more.

"So tonight was real to you? I mean, what happened on the overlook," she asked weakly.

"Alex and I were told by our handler that if we didn't complete the job, then it would be done by another and we would be the next targets. I know this is a huge shock to you, but I want you to know that if we would have just left then you would be dead and we would be on the run. On the other hand, if I would have killed you like I was supposed to, then I would not be able to live much longer anyway."

"What are you saying," Cady said shocked.

"It's weird, I know that you and I just met, and not exactly under the best circumstances, but for me, it's like my eyes just opened. I didn't want to kill you, exactly the opposite. Tonight I made the decision to protect you at all costs, and even if you don't want my help, that is exactly what I will do."

Cady looked as if she were going to cry and Gabriel knew that he was the cause of it. It hurt him to see her in pain, mental or physical.

"Gabe, I know you're here to help and I appreciate it, but this is a lot to take in. I only wish this hadn't happened. I just don't know what to think anymore. Gabriel, I hate what you are.

"I hate what I am too, trust me."

The door opened and Alex stood in the entryway. Looking around the yard and across the street, he looked disturbed.

"What's wrong," asked Gabriel.

Alex turned toward Gabriel and with a worried smile; he threw a small piece of paper onto Gabriel lap. Gabriel picked up the note and unfolded it.

Got your message, I agree Gabriel will be too much for one person to handle, I'll see you at 12:00 tonight, be careful brother.

Gabriel crinkled the note and dropped it to the ground.

"Alex, what time is it"

"Midnight," he said quietly.

Chapter 21
Injured

In a flash Gabriel jumped off of the swing and pulled Cady up with him. Dragging her through the door and hurrying toward the kitchen where they had left Martin Bishop, Cady began to resist.

"Gabe, what the hell is going on," she said outraged.

Gabriel didn't respond, instead he kept dragging her toward the kitchen where her father sat shakily drinking his coffee. Looking up as the two assassins holding his daughter entered the kitchen, Martin looked confused.

"What is the meaning of this," Martin said angrily.

"Get up Mr. Bishop, it's time to leave," said Alex quickly.

"I'll do no such thing. My daughter and I are staying in this house until my security team gets here."

"Trust me Mr. Bishop, they are no match for what is about to come down on us," retorted Gabriel as Cady was still trying to break loose from his grip.

"What do you mean," asked Bishop.

"There is someone else here, we need to leave now," said Gabriel as he grabbed his leather jacket from the back of the chair. "Cady, you and your father need to pack one bag each, we won't be coming back here. Alex, I need you to scout the bottom floor, we're leaving in five."

Alex nodded and moved from the kitchen to the hallway with caution. Drawing his weapon, Alex disappeared around the corner of the next room.

Entering the living room, Alex pointed his weapon at each corner checking for possible threats. *I wonder which one came with Raphael, he usually works alone,* he thought. *Raphael was good, but he was no match for Gabriel and he knew that; maybe that's why he brought someone else.* Alex spotted movement near the couch on the far end of the living room. Moving slowly, he placed his back along the brick fireplace on the left wall and continued to move forward with his weapon raised. Trying to see around the couch was an impossibility, not an ideal place for an assassin to conceal himself, but somewhat effective. Alex swept the remainder of the room with his peripheral vision, keeping his eyes on the couch. With his back still to the wall, he came to an entryway and quickly moved his head in and out, checking for possible ambush locations, but found nothing. Moving away from the wall, he tightened his grip on the pistol and rushed to side of the couch for a clear view of the assailant. Looking down at the bare floor, he was confused. Seconds earlier he could have sworn that he saw movement. Turning away, he moved back into the hallway connecting to the kitchen and saw Gabriel with his weapon drawn as well. Standing in front of Cady to protect her, he shot an inquisitive look at Alex.

"We are clear," shouted Alex.

Gabriel nodded and turned back to Cady and her father giving them the signal to move. The three of them raced up the stairs and into their respective bedrooms. Gabriel followed Cady since she was the primary target. She grabbed a small backpack from under her bed and began tossing clothes into it.

"Gabe, do I have time to change out of this dress," she asked.

"Not really, but you're going to have to. I need you in something comfortable in case we have to run."

Cady ran into her private bathroom and closed the door. Gabriel moved to the window of her room and peered outside. *Looks quiet,* he thought. Knowing that sight was not something to rely on with assassins of this caliber, he dismissed the thought that they would be able to escape without a confrontation.

Cady exited the bathroom in a pair of jeans and a blue sweatshirt. Sliding in her tennis shoes, she nodded to Gabriel that she was ready. As they left the bedroom, Gabriel spotted Martin walking down the hall toward Cady's room.

"Are you ok honey," he asked.

"I'm fine," she said shakily.

Gabriel led the way to the bottom of the stairs and looked at Alex once more for confirmation that the house was still clear. With a nod, Gabriel motioned for everyone to leave the house together.

Cady and Martin both understood the signal and grabbed their belongings before moving back behind Gabriel. They moved down the hallway toward Alex with Gabriel in the lead. Alex waited until they passed and took up the rear as they moved for the front door. Gabriel turned the knob and slowly pulled the door open checking for possible hostiles. Peering out into the darkness, Gabriel could see nothing that posed a threat and opened the door the rest of the way.

As the foursome stepped out into the cool night air, Gabriel gave a hand signal to Alex to sweep the yard. Alex moved into the yard quickly with his back turned to the driveway where Gabriel was now aiming his weapon. Gabriel waved for Martin and Cady to follow him as he neared Bishop's SUV. Clicking open the back door, Gabriel turned toward Cady and her father.

"Get in and keep your heads down."

Martin nodded and helped Cady into the vehicle then climbed in behind her. Gabriel removed a small device from his jacket that Alex recognized as an explosive detector. Powering on the device he heard the detector begin to click which meant would mean that the vehicle was clear. He moved it along the bottom of the vehicle and tires, and then swept it over the hood. Gabriel was nearly satisfied with the readings of the explosive detector when it sounded a small wail. Gabriel's eyes widened and he rushed back to the rear door of the SUV and flung it open.

"GET OUT," he shouted.

Martin jumped out of his seat and onto the driveway tuning to help Cady but Gabriel was already in front of him grabbing his daughter by the waist and yanking her from the vehicle. Alex reached out and took Bishop by the shoulder, leading him away from the vehicle. Cady was now being carried by Gabriel as he ran from the black SUV. He only made it ten feet from the vehicle before a large explosion deafened the sound of everything else. Feeling the heat and shock of the explosion Gabriel was thrown forward onto the ground with Cady flying from his arms.

Gabriel landed hard on the front lawn knocking the wind from his lungs. Disoriented, he tried to stand bout found that he couldn't. Cady lay in front of Gabriel looking into his eyes with fear. Still unable to concentrate, Alex rushed to his side obviously unaffected by the explosion. Kneeling beside Gabriel, Alex quickly checked his partner for injuries. When he neared Gabriel's left shoulder, he saw the reason that he could not stand. A large piece of shrapnel from the vehicle was lodged just below the shoulder, still smoking. Sweeping his weapon around the front of the house again, Alex still saw nothing to indicate that someone was hiding in the shadows.

"Gabe, can you move at all," Alex asked hurriedly.

"No, my legs are too weak.

Alex moved his right hand over the shrapnel still using his left to sweep the yard with his weapon. In the chaos, Gabriel did not see Cady move beside Alex and kneel.

"Cady, I need you to pull that piece of metal out of his back," said Alex.

"But, I don't think I can."

"No buts," Alex retorted. "Either you get it out of him or we all die here."

Looking distressed, Cady moved her hands to the shrapnel but did not attempt to pull it out. Realizing that she was having second thoughts about removing the object from his back, Gabriel reached out and put his hand on her knee.

"It's ok," Gabriel reassured her.

Cady nodded as a tear fell from her cheek. She put both hands on the object and pulled as hard as she could. The object came out without much force. Gabriel had expected a great deal more pain, but this was manageable.

"Martin, help Cady get him up, we have to move," commanded Alex.

Martin moved to the right side of Gabriel and Cady grabbed his left arm. They hoisted him up and placed each of his arms around their necks. Alex stood at Cady's side and started directing them toward their apartment.

"Behind the building is our vehicle. We need to reach it before whoever is out here makes himself known."

Cady and Martin helped Gabriel walk toward the apartment building. Crossing the street, Alex still saw nothing to give away the hitters position. *This is weird, if he knows Gabriel is down, why isn't he attacking,* he asked himself. Cady and Martin now reached the right side of the building and began walking Gabriel down the small pathway leading to his vehicle. As they made their way through the tight space between the apartment building and a wooden fence, Alex again thought he spotted movement near the end of the hall. Taking the lead, he raised his weapon toward the source of the movement. Shadows crept across the wall as if trying to distract him from a potential target. Coming to the end of the passage Alex spotted the vehicle sitting where Gabriel had left it only an hour before.

Gabriel felt extremely weak; there was no possible way for him to defend Cady or her father by himself. He was grateful that he had Alex's' loyalty. Alex had taken the lead and had proven to be the best asset he had in this fight. Looking toward his partner, he saw a look of concern on his face.

"What's wrong Alex," Gabriel asked weakly.

"The vehicle is fifty feet to the North," Alex said pointing straight toward it.

"So what's the problem," chimed Cady.

"From the look on Alex's face, so is the hitter," Gabriel answered for his partner.

Alex simply nodded trying not to give away his position since he was in the lead of the extraction. Gabriel turned and began examining the fence for a weak point that they could perhaps use to crawl through in the hopes of flanking the hitter but found nothing.

"This is a really bad position Gabe, we are sitting ducks here," said Alex.

Gabriel nodded but before he could figure out a way to get them all out safely, he heard a familiar voice coming from the direction of the vehicle.

"Gabriel and Alex, I know you're in the walkway. Please step out, I mean you no harm," said a very calm voice.

Gabriel was surprised to hear those words. Not only had they helped their target to escape, but killed Raphael in the process. By all that he knew, every member of the Choir would want him dead. Alex turned to Gabriel again, this time with a look of confusion on his face.

"Jeremiel," Alex asked. Gabriel simply nodded at him.

"What do we do," asked Cady.

"We show ourselves," answered Gabriel.

Gabriel noticed glances of anger and confusion from all three of the people with him. Even Alex was not ready to accept that Jeremiel meant them no harm. Gabriel raised his weapon and signaled Alex to follow him out of the small entryway. Moving in unison the two men pointed their weapons directly at Jeremiel who was now standing in the open leaning against Gabriel's SUV. Jeremiel spotted Gabriel and Alex immediately and raised his hands in surrender.

"I'm not here to hurt you guys," said Jeremiel calmly.

Gabriel knew that Jeremiel was the best at keeping his cool in tense situations and was the first to act rationally when the adrenaline started pumping. Still pointing their weapons at the would-be killer, Gabriel was the first to approach him.

"How did you get here so quickly Jeremi," asked Gabriel forcefully.

Jeremiel had always liked the shortened name that Gabriel had given him. He also knew that Gabriel was trying to appeal to him not to make a sudden movement.

"Marcus," answered Jeremiel.

"Marcus said that he only sent Raphael," Alex retorted.

"Of course he would say that. He didn't want you both to know that two more of us were here in the event that you did manage to kill Raphael. Marcus knew that Raphael was no match for you Gabriel; he also knew that you would turn against us."

"Jeremi, who is the third hitter," asked Gabriel weakly, barely able to keep his weapon trained on his target.

"It was Danyel," Jeremiel said with a smile.

"What do you mean was," asked Alex.

"I apologize for not stopping him sooner, but until we arrived here to see you exiting the target's house, we had no idea that it was you Gabriel. Marcus simply told us that an agent had gone rogue and we were to stop him. When I saw you two protecting the targets it was too late for me to stop Danyel from detonating the car bomb, but I did manage to silence him shortly thereafter."

"Danyel is dead," asked Gabriel.

Jeremiel simply nodded with his usual confidence. Gabriel knew that he could trust Jeremiel, especially when he gave that nod. If there was one flaw with his old trainee, it was that he was cocky and liked to brag about his kills.

"What are your intentions Jeremi," asked Gabriel skeptically.

"I figure that you saved my life while I was in training twice, I owe you this much at least."

"First of all it was three times that I saved your ass," Gabriel laughed weakly. "You know that Marcus will have you killed for helping us."

"Not if you overpowered me upon your escape," said Jeremiel with his confident smile. "Just make it look good."

Gabriel looked at Jeremiel and nodded. Jeremiel turned around with his arms raised. Gabriel mustered all of his remaining power and struck Jeremiel on the back of the head with his weapon. Jeremiel instantly crumpled onto the ground unconscious. Gabriel turned back to Cady and Martin motioning for them to get into the SUV. It was time to make tracks and Gabriel knew that other members of the Choir would be close behind.

Chapter 22
Safe House

After driving for several hours, Alex finally pulled into a safe house that he and Gabriel had set up in case the authorities ever identified them. Laying low here would be easy considering that nobody knew of the safe house but Gabriel and Alex. Martin Bishop was riding shotgun with Gabriel lying across Cady's lap in the back. Over the past hour Gabriel had begun to spike a fever which was a sign of infection. Alex had decided to use the safe house until Gabriel was on his feet but he couldn't tell how long that would be. Since leaving the small town of Shaver Lake Martin Bishop had not said a word. Alex could hear Cady speaking quietly to Gabriel in the back seat but couldn't tell what she was saying.

Stepping out of the vehicle, Alex stretched his legs and walked onto the front porch of the safe house. He surveyed their surroundings and found no possible ambush points in the area. The safe house was approximately one mile back into the forest and the property was covered with trees. Although it may prove a disadvantage for them if they were found, there would be no way for someone to enter the property unnoticed. Thinking back to when he and Gabriel had purchased the house, Gabriel explained to Alex the sounds of the animals in the forest would be the best natural alarm that one can get.

Walking back to the vehicle he opened the door for Martin Bishop then Cady. She was sitting upright with a look of concern on her face which Alex could tell was due to Gabriel's injury.

"Let's get him into the house and let him rest while I patch the wound," said Alex.

"Alex is he going to be ok," asked Cady.

"Gabe is a tough guy, he will be fine once we treat the injury," Alex said.

Reassuring Cady was probably not the best idea, especially if Gabriel died but he really had no choice. Keeping Cady and her father calm was better than the alternative. Grabbing Gabriel under each arm, Alex helped him out of the vehicle and into the house with Cady and her father following close behind. The foursome entered the living room and placed Gabriel on the brown sofa. Looking around, Alex had forgotten how nice the safe house really was. They had purchased the house two years ago and moved in some equipment then never returned.

For a reason that Alex could not imagine, it was fairly cold in the old house although outside it was eighty-five degrees. He walked over to the small fireplace situated on the far left wall of the living room. The logs that he had placed there two years ago sat untouched in the same place he had left them. Alex pulled some old newspaper that was sitting near the logs and placed it along the bottom of the fireplace. He then chose several medium sized logs and built a small pyramid over the newspaper. Lighting the ends of the paper, he soon had a crackling fire to warm the house. He pulled the fire poker from its stand on the right side of the fireplace and shuffled the logs accordingly so that they would not roll onto the carpet. Alex heard Gabriel moan as he switched positions on the sofa. He dropped the poker into the fire and hurried to his partner's side.

Kneeling beside Gabriel to check his wound, Alex could sense that he was in a great deal of pain by the way he clenched his teeth every time he moved. Rolling Gabriel onto his side, Alex saw that the wound was located below Gabriel's left shoulder blade. The wound was fairly deep but Alex was optimistic about being able to treat the wound. Turning to Cady with an expression of relief, Alex began directing her on where to find the items that he needed to close the wound.

"Upstairs in the first closet on the left there is an emergency medical bag. I will need that as well as several bath towels and hot water," commanded Alex.

Cady nodded and ran upstairs to find the supplies that they needed. Alex continued to hold Gabriel in place. Martin Bishop stood over the two boys examining the wound for himself. He didn't seem to be disturbed at the sight of blood, which Alex guessed was due to his trip to China. Seeing your partner die and being shot yourself can really toughen someone up.

"Will he be alright," asked Martin.

"He's had worse, this shouldn't be a problem," explained Alex.

"Worse, are you kidding me? This wound looks like it should have killed him."

"Mr. Bishop, Gabriel has been shot twice, stabbed once, and mauled by a lion, this is nothing."

"MAULED BY A LION? You have got to be kidding me!"

"Yea, I'm kidding," Alex chuckled.

Alex could have gone on but he heard Gabriel begin to laugh and knew that it pained him to do so.

"You boys are sick," responded Bishop.

Alex was glad that he could lighten the mood a little but quickly remembered that is was time to help his partner when he saw Cady descending the stairs in a hurry. She brought the medical bag and towels placing them beside Alex.

"I still need hot water, I'll be in the kitchen," she said.

Alex opened the medical bag and found the antibiotics and stitching equipment. Opening the package he saw Gabriel try to turn his head around to see what was going on.

"Sit still you silly asshole or you'll tear your wound open even more," quipped Alex.

Alex began to thread the needle but was stopped by Gabriel who had laid his hand on Alex's shoulder.

"We don't have time for stitches," said Gabriel.

"I thought you might say that," retorted Alex. "You sure about this?"

"As sure as I'm going to be," responded Gabriel.

Cady returned from the kitchen as Alex was stirring the fire again. She placed the hot water next to the sofa where Gabriel was laying. She brushed some of his hair off of his forehead noticing that he was burning up. Feeling his forehead again she guessed his temperature at well over 101 degrees. She reached into the medical kit that Alex had asked for. Pulling out a large brown bottle of peroxide she unscrewed the cap and poured some over Gabriel's wound. Cady saw the bubbling begin in his back and was surprised to see how dirty the wound really was. She turned to look at Alex whom she thought was still standing at the fireplace but only saw the fiery glow of the flames jumping up toward the chimney.

Where in the world is Alex, she thought as she turned back to Gabriel. Before she could look again she heard Alex re-entering the room behind her. Out of the corner of her eye, her father had moved to the edge of his seat looking angry.

"Your partner is injured and you're drinking," questioned her father angrily.

Cady turned around to look at Alex who was now holding a bottle of Jack Daniels whiskey. She was no drinker but knew that this was some pretty powerful stuff.

"It's not for me," retorted Alex as he sat down beside Cady and handed to bottle to his injured partner. "Drink up."

Cady looked in awe at Gabriel who had grabbed the bottle and started pounding the liquid down his throat.

"Thirsty," she asked as she touched his forehead again.

"Not exactly," Gabriel responded weakly.

Alex had pulled a syringe and a vial of antibiotic from the medical bag and was drawing up a dose for Gabriel. Cady watched as he swabbed Gabriel's arm and jabbed the needle into his vein.

"This should help with the infection," said Alex. "With any luck the fever will break overnight."

Gabriel nodded and took another swig of the whiskey before rolling onto his other side clearly exposing the wound. Alex walked back to the fireplace and grabbed the long iron poker that he had left in the fire. Glowing red, the poker made its way at the hand of Alex back to the sofa.

Holding the poker near Gabriel's wound he began to ask Gabriel if he was ready but was stopped short by Cady.

"ARE YOU KIDDING ME? You can't burn him with that," she yelled.

Alex looked a little dazed at what she had said. He looked up to Martin Bishop who obviously understood what was going on. Martin nodded his head and moved closer to Gabriel grabbing him by the legs and holding him down.

"Cady, I've got his shoulders, you just hold his hand if that's ok," said Alex.

Cady nodded and grabbed Gabriel's hand with a tears forming in her eyes. Up until now she felt numb at tonight's events but now was feeling as though she might lose her best friend. It was odd for her to use such a term for Gabriel, but even though he was sent to kill her, he really had turned into her best friend.

"You ready," Alex asked Gabriel.

"Do it," Gabriel said with a rush of vigor, which Alex knew was a combination of alcohol and adrenaline.

Alex leaned in and pressed the still red hot poker into Gabriel's wound. The sound of searing flesh made Cady and her father look away but Alex held firm. He could see Gabriel stirring and held his shoulder even more firmly than before. Gabriel let out a deafening yell as Alex continued to cauterize his wound. Gabriel could only see the backing of the sofa as the searing pain struck him in a seemingly never ending flurry of pain. He could feel the weight of Martin Bishop and Alex holding him down, but the most comforting fact was the light touch he felt in his hands. It was Cady, holding him with a reassuring grip. After only ten seconds, the pressure finally left his wound and he knew that it was over. The pain was still unbearable. The last thing Gabriel would see was the pitch black of the inside of his own eyelids as he was rendered unconscious from the pain.

Chapter 23
Finding a Reason

Cady tossed and turned in bed for an hour before finally getting frustrated and walking out of the guest room. She walked down the stairs of the small safe house that Gabriel and Alex had brought her to three hours ago. The night was much too exciting to be able to sleep even a wink so far. Not only had she found out that the man that she thought she loved turned out to be an assassin who was sent to kill her, but he had murdered a man right in front of her eyes. She was certainly not expecting to see anything like this in her life time, but here she was smack dab in the middle of it. She walked into the small kitchen to make herself a cup of coffee but found that Alex was already pouring a second cup near the counter.

"I heard you get up. Figured that you could use this," Alex said handing the steaming cup to Cady.

Cady smiled and took a seat at the kitchen table beside Alex. He was apparently working vigilantly with his laptop as he didn't show the signs of exhaustion that Cady was. Looking around the small kitchen, she was slightly disgusted at the shape of the room. Although she didn't expect the safe house to be anything near what she was used to but peeling yellow paint, soot covered linoleum, and a rusted gas stove was a little too unsanitary for her taste. Alex seemed to sense her disgust and also took a look around the room.

"Needs some work huh," he said with a smile.

"I feel like I need a tetanus shot just sitting in here," Cady retorted.

"When Gabe and I bought this place, we just tossed some equipment in the closets and left it as it was. This was only designed to be a safe house for just such an occasion."

"So you thought something like this might happen?"

"Not exactly," said Alex. "We had originally purchased this house to lay low in the event that one or both of us were caught on camera by the police. If the police were after us, the Choir would not give us shelter. If you remember those old Mission Impossible movies, they delete your files and you're on your own."

"That's kind of odd, you would think that these people would help you so that you didn't get arrested and talk to the police," said Cady.

"Chances are, if you were arrested, that you would never make it to questioning alive. The Choir would see to that."

Cady took a sip of her coffee and it seemed to relax her for a second, but reality struck and she thought again about the trouble that she was in. She decided to concentrate on helping Alex to take her mind off of things.

"What are you working on," asked Cady.

Alex continued typing on the laptop and concentrating on the screen. Without taking his eyes away, he began to explain what he was doing.

"I'm working on hacking the Choir's database. This will let me know which member is assigned to take us out. It can potentially give us a way to elude them for the time being."

"For the time being," asked Cady.

"We can't hide from them forever, eventually they will find us."

"So what do we do when they do find us," she asked.

"Try not to die," retorted Alex.

Cady stirred in her seat. That comment made her think of death and how very close she had come tonight. She was hoping for a solid answer like changing identities or leaving the country, but Alex made it seem like these people can find you anywhere.

"You should get some sleep," said Alex looking up from the computer screen.

"I can't, too much has happened tonight; too much to think about."

"I'm sensing that you're not talking about our grand escape tonight," responded Alex.

"Well I am, but I've been thinking of other things too."

"Gabriel," Alex asked silently.

"Yea, is it that obvious," Cady asked with a pause. "I really liked him, and he turned out to be a murderer. I don't think that I can ever look at him the same again. I know he saved my life twice tonight, but it's the whole contract killer thing that I can't deal with."

Alex looked at Cady as if he were deciding to tell her something important. With a small sigh, he moved his chair closer to Cady and put his hand on her shoulder.

"Look, it's not that Gabriel and I were killing people for fun. We also never killed anyone who didn't deserve it. I know that is getting into semantics about who really deserves to die, but it's the truth. Everyone we have ever taken out was a really bad person. Murderers, rapists, slave traders; hell we were even contracted by the U.S. Government to track and kill a serial killer once. Listen Cady, I know that what I'm saying probably doesn't mean much to you in the way of justifying what we do, but I want you to know that Gabriel had been conflicted about this job since he first met you. Once he found out you were innocent, he pretty much decided to protect you from that point forward."

"Alex, I hear what you're saying, but..." Cady trailed off.

"No buts, just read this and you will understand everything," Alex said as he slid the laptop across the table so that Cady could see clearly. "If this doesn't change your mind then I am sure Gabriel will understand. He certainly would never want you to see this but I think it's only right for you to know how he feels about you."

Alex got up from his chair and walked out of the kitchen into the living room and knelt beside his unconscious partner. Cady suspected that he was talking to him as they did appear very close, but figured that it was more for Alex's piece of mind and that Gabriel probably couldn't hear him. Turning her attention to the laptop, Cady scrolled to the top and found that this was a log that Gabriel had written while he was with Cady. She began reading and found the information to be really dry. It seemed that Gabriel was using this as a report to his superiors for the time he spent watching her.

12, June 2010

Target was first spotted at the Shaver Lake Mall. The mark appeared to be with an acquaintance or friend. We were successful in the acquisition of the Marks credit cards and photo identification. We will attempt to run all known contacts through the database as well as build a database of all acquaintances and relationships in which to have a better understanding of our target and her habits. Termination date is yet unknown, however, we should have an accurate estimate on the next status report.

13, June 2010

Alexander was assigned to watch the mark and to keep her distracted long enough to plant bugging equipment in her residence. I successfully placed camera equipment and listening devices in every room including all land line phones. Gaining access to the marks personal laptop was an added bonus. Recorded: Firefly1284 as the marks password to her personal laptop, banking accounts, and email. Through the laptop I was able to clone the marks phone so that any calls made can be heard through my direct line.

14, June 2010

Marcus,

Something is wrong with this assignment. I have combed through the marks personal banking accounts, e-mail, and phone messages. The mark seems to be a normal teenage girl. What has she done wrong to have me waste my time on this? Do you really need a 1ˢᵗ Class member on this? We need to talk, get back to me.

15, June 2010

It turns out that Cady is a normal teenage girl after all. I am disappointed to know that I was sent here for this. Cady Bishop is a nice girl in every respect and completely innocent from any wrongdoing, especially something that would have targeted her with the company. It seems as though I need to re-evaluate my stance on just doing the job and going home. I had to protect this girl from a drunken idiot that was trying to hurt her. Not only did I protect her from this, but it felt good in the process. Protecting an innocent is not something I am used to, but it gave me a better feeling than terminating those that would do harm to others.

It seems as though protecting Cady is something that I am meant to do. I stopped that guy from hitting her last night, and this evening I find an assassin moving around in her house. I put two bullets in his head and cleaned up the mess. Perhaps I am meant to be her guardian angel after all?

15, June 2010

Cady asked me on a date a few minutes ago. After spending time with this girl, I have realized what part I am to play in life. I have saved her life already, and I may just do it again. Marcus gave us the green light and also notified me that if the girl was not taken out tonight, Alex and I would also suffer her fate. I know what I have to do, but what am I truly supposed to do? Marcus knows that I am against the killing of innocents so why would he even send me here? I have to make a decision, a decision that will determine not only the fate of Cady Bishop, but that of Alex and me as well. I get the sense that Alex would not argue with me if I didn't kill her, but I'm conflicted. Do I sign a death warrant for my best friend, or the girl that I think I have fallen in love with? I will make my decision tonight...Only time will tell.

Cady could not believe what she had read. He was not only going to kill her, but do it on their first date. She tried to think back to the time they had spent together, but found that her memory was blocked by some weird feeling that she couldn't describe. The only things that were flashing through her mind were her kiss with Gabriel, the man trying to kill her, and their escape. Everything else was just a haze of speeding memory that she couldn't slow down.

One thing kept drawing her eyes back to the last paragraph of Gabriel's report. She focused in on the last part of one of the sentences. *"The girl that I think I have fallen in love with."* Cady was in shock and awe at the statement. Up until a few hours ago, she had felt the same way about Gabriel. They had only known each other for just over a week and they were both in love. Cady lowered her head into her hands and tried to make sense of it all. She couldn't really figure out what she was feeling, but she knew that Gabriel was in love with her, as she had hoped in the past. What was she feeling for him now, knowing what she does about him? She still had the same feeling that she had in the past. She thought that she might love him but it was just much more complicated than before. Now they were all running for their lives, did she really have time for love, or should she embrace it because they may not have much time left together?

Cady's head was reeling. She stood up from the chair and walked into the living room where Gabriel still lay on the sofa. He was in the same position that he was when he lost consciousness. She sat down beside the sofa and began to examine his wound. The large burn under the gauze was almost completely visible. She guessed that it would heal, but could not imagine the amount of pain Gabriel was in because of her. It hit her for the first time since this disastrous night had started. She knew now that she was glad to have Gabriel here. It wasn't his fault that her father had messed up and almost got her killed. She was glad that Gabriel had come to know her and that it wasn't the man whom Gabriel had shot. If he had been sent alone, she would already be dead. *Gabriel is truly my guardian angel,* she thought. *But since he has fallen from grace from the Choir, perhaps it is better for me to call him my Fallen Angel.*

Chapter 24
Back to Work

Gabriel awoke to a massive pain below his left shoulder. It took him a moment to remember all that had happened last night. If it weren't for Alex, that piece of shrapnel would certainly have killed him. Raising his hand to his forehead, he noticed that his fever had broken sometime during the night thanks to the antibiotics. Gabriel rolled over on the sofa so that he was facing the room instead of staring at the back of the large brown couch. Looking down to the floor he spotted Cady, sound asleep beside him. *Why in the world she didn't sleep in bed*, he wondered. Sitting up and stretching his arms outward, the pain shot up into his shoulder and down into his lower back. The wound would heal but Gabriel had no time to sit idly by and wait to be back at 100%. Gabriel silently stood up trying not to wake Cady, but when he took his first step forward he accidentally bumped her and she stirred and awoke.

"Sorry, I didn't mean to wake you," said Gabriel looking down at Cady.

"It's cool," she said. "Should you be on your feet? It might be better if you take some time to rest."

Gabriel contemplated what she had said; it would certainly be nice to rest for a few more days but he didn't have the luxury of resting. Gabriel was sure that by now Marcus had found out what had transpired and has already reassigned several more members to clean up the mess. They would be actively looking for everyone in this safe house, and when they found them, it would most certainly be a bloodbath. He watched as Cady picked herself up off of the floor. *Laying there in that old red carpet can't be very comfortable. I wonder why she fell asleep there*, he thought.

"I need to keep moving around," Gabriel began. "If I don't then my muscles near the wound will tighten and I will be no good to anyone. Not to mention I can't sit on the sofa all day, I would go insane."

Cady smiled and began walking with Gabriel into the kitchen. They both pulled out a chair in at the table and sat down. Alex, who was preparing breakfast moved to his left and grabbed several coffee cups and placed them on the kitchen table.

"Good to see you up and about," said Alex.

Gabriel simply smiled and went back to looking at Cady. He had hoped that if he stared at her enough that he could figure out if she would ever forgive him. Gabriel came to the conclusion that it would be impossible to tell what Cady was thinking after all that had happened, and figured that he should just ask her, but not here in front of Alex.

Gabriel and Alex both heard Martin Bishop walking down the stairs. When Bishop rounded the corner, Alex was already setting a place for him.

"Morning," said Alex.

"Good morning everyone," Martin said as he sat down.

"You sure are cheerful today Dad," said Cady.

"Well, we are alive aren't we? Every day is a good day when you're still alive," quipped Martin.

The four of them sat and ate their breakfast without saying a word to each other. Gabriel and Alex both guessed that Cady and her father were still taking in what was truly happening so they decided not to interject until they were ready to hear the next move.

After breakfast, Martin stayed at the kitchen table drinking another cup of coffee while Alex cleaned the dishes. Cady moved to help Alex by drying the plates while Gabriel began gathering their equipment that they had left two years ago. In the closet, he found the duffel bags exactly where they had left them. The first duffel that Gabriel unzipped contained two laptops and surveillance equipment. The second was loaded with weapons of every kind. Gabriel knew that if they were found, they would have one hell of a time fending off an attack. If Marcus had sent more than one 1st class agent, then they were doomed, but we would fight to the last breath to protect Cady.

Several minutes later, Gabriel had one of the laptops up and running. All that was left to do was place the surveillance cameras and motion detectors. He gathered up all of the components that he needed and headed for the door. As he opened the door, he found Cady entering the foyer from the bathroom to the right of the door.

"Where are you going," she asked silently.

Gabriel knew that she was still broken up from the events of last night, and probably had a hard time talking to him without showing anger or hate toward him. He decided to make his response short and sweet.

"I need to place these cameras on the perimeter so we know if anyone is trying to sneak up on us."

"Oh," Cady said. "Need some help?"

Gabriel smiled at her. He wanted to decline her offer but couldn't bring himself to deny spending any time with her.

"Sure, if you don't mind," he responded.

Gabriel handed Cady half of the equipment and they proceeded out the door and into the front yard, which was more like a forest. They walked about 50 feet and Gabriel moved toward a large pine tree which lay directly in front of the house. He examined the tree for a second and determined that this was a good spot for a camera or two. He pulled nearby log to the tree and stepped up on it wincing at his sore back. Cady handed him the first camera and he affixed it as high as he could possibly get it. Next he activated a motion detector beside the camera. He knew that even if they weren't monitoring the screens then the motion detectors would certainly let them know if there were any unwanted guests.

For the next thirty minutes Gabriel and Cady walked the perimeter and installed the surveillance equipment. *About halfway done,* Gabriel thought. He looked at Cady who was standing close still holding the remaining cameras. She was smiling at Gabriel, and that was something he certainly did not expect. Gabriel smiled back and slowly walked over to where she stood.

"What are you smiling at," Gabriel asked.

"You," was all she said.

"Why me; I thought I'd never see you smile again."

"I never thought I would smile again either." She said as the smile began to fade. "Listen Gabe, I know we still have some work to do but can we stop and talk for a minute?

"Sure," he said. "Let's sit here and you can tell me what is on your mind."

Cady cracked another smile as they moved under the tree that they just installed a camera on and sat. Cady put the cameras on the ground and turned back to Gabriel. She stared into his green eyes again, which amazed Gabriel because not only did she have the same color eyes, but it was as if all of her anger was gone and she was back to showing her interest in him. He couldn't help but stare back into her eyes with the same distinction and wonder that she was thinking.

"So what's on your mind," asked Gabriel.

"I wanted to thank you for everything you have done for my father and me."

"You mean spying on you, following you, and trying to kill you," he retorted harshly.

"Gabe, I know that you are being really hard on yourself and there really is no need. I may be a teenage girl but I'm not stupid. If you weren't there, we would have died. It's not your fault and it's not my fathers' fault. It's the people that got us into this in the first place."

"You mean the CIA," Gabriel asked.

"Yes, them and that Chinese guy that hired you. It's their fault and nobody else's. Gabe, I am glad that I met you and I am glad that you are who you are, because it wasn't for you, I would be dead."

"Cady, it's complicated. I know that you are probably glad that I am around for now, but this is my fault. If there weren't people like me out there then you would be in no danger."

"But there are people like you, and I for one am grateful that at least three of you exist that try to make the world a better place. Alex told me that you did this not only because I haven't done anything wrong, but that you were falling in love with me. That tells me that there is something immensely good in you; at least you have more good than bad. I want you to know that I trust you."

Gabriel contemplated what Cady had just said. He closed his eyes and tried to think of all of the murders he had committed in the name of peace but everything seemed to have lost its meaning. *Perhaps I am nothing but a common murderer,* he thought to himself.

"How can you trust me when you don't even know me Cady? I have done some really bad things in my life, and now that I look back at these things, I wish that I could take it all back." Gabriel looked deep into Cady's eyes again. "The really evil part of me isn't even sorry for who I killed and what I have done to people. My biggest regret is lying to you."

"Well I have a good idea Gabe," she said looking down at the ground which Gabriel recognized as one of those embarrassed girl poses.

"What's your good idea," he asked with a skeptical tone.

"I think we should start over as if we have never met before. That way I can get to know the real Gabriel."

"Interesting idea," said Gabriel. "But how is it that you can forget what I tried to do to you? If anything I am the villain in this story."

"Are you kidding me? Gabe, you're a hero, not a villain. Did you actually try to kill me, or did you save my life Gabe? I'm not pretending to understand everything that has gone on in the last week but what I do understand is that I am grateful that you are with me. You saved my life more than once, pissed off some of the most powerful people in the world, and basically signed your own death warrant by defending me. To me, that is very heroic, and worthy of my forgiveness. You just have to promise to always tell me the truth from now on."

"I can do that," he said.

Gabriel cracked a smile at Cady. He didn't want to seem excited like a teenage boy so on the outside he kept his cool but inside of his head he was doing back flips. Cady was the one person in the world that not only made Gabriel change his ways, but ironically, she made him feel safe. He was now sure that she felt the same way about him. *Perhaps this really is love,* he thought. Standing up and facing Cady, he reached out and helped her up.

"Hello, my name is Gabriel Mason. I'm twenty three years old, have never been in a relationship that wasn't a total lie, and I'm an assassin sent here to kill you. Unfortunately for me, I can't seem to harm a hair on your head because I seem to have fallen for you."

"Nice to meet you Gabriel, my name is Cady Bishop. I'm nineteen years old, have also never been in a relationship that wasn't a total lie, and even though you were sent here to kill me, I trust you with my life."

"Is this the part where I get to kiss you," asked Gabriel

"Sorry sir, I don't kiss on the first date."

"Since when," he asked.

"Since now, I have a new outlook on dating. You like it?"

"Not really. But does this at least count as our first date?"

"Nope," she said with a coy smile.

"So now you're playing hard to get," Gabriel asked with an inquisitive look.

"Always," retorted Cady with the same smile that Gabriel had fallen in love with.

"So when do I get to take you on a date," he asked. "I mean a real date, one where I won't try to kill you."

"Tomorrow, pick me up around six," said Cady smiling even bigger than before.

Cady began walking away, leaving Gabriel to complete the rest of his work. He watched her until she entered the house and went back to hanging the surveillance equipment with a renewed vigor. *Tomorrow will definitely be interesting,* he thought.

Chapter 25
Warzone

.

FBI Agent Kristen Shamhat walked the perimeter of what could have been a warzone. She had not yet presented herself to the local Sheriff who was running the investigation. She liked having the freedom of walking in the crowd of onlookers taking in the sights that they saw before getting the whole story. It was easier for her this way, milling through the rubberneckers; talking to them as f she were just another citizen. Frequently when she questioned witnessed or suspects they were reluctant to give up the information that she needed, this way, it was as if the individuals she spoke to couldn't help but speculate to her what had happened. *A different approach with a fresh set of eyes is sometimes all you need,* she thought.

The large house, which she had estimated to have cost Martin Bishop several million dollars, was completely burnt to the ground. Casualty reports stated that there were three dead but none were Bishop or his daughter Cady. As she continued to wander through the crowd, she eyed every visible corner of the property sizing up the crime scene from her point of view. No doubt this was a professional hit from the looks of what had happened here.

As she neared the eastern part of Martin Bishop's property, she found a distraught girl looking at the house with such longing that she could only have been a close friend or relative. Agent Shamhat approached the tall blond at a slow pace, trying not to give herself away as an FBI agent. She stood beside the girl for a moment before speaking.

"What a shame; was anybody hurt," asked Agent Shamhat already knowing the answer.

The young girl sniffled and looked at Agent Shamhat, sizing her up before responding.

"I'm not sure, but my best friend lived here and I haven't been able to reach her since I found out."

"Oh, who is your best friend," questioned Agent Shamhat gently.

"Her name was Cady Bishop. She and I knew each other since kindergarten. Her father owned a large computer business in L.A."

Large computer business, thought Agent Shamhat, *What an understatement. Martin Bishop was the second largest producer of silicon computer chips in the United States.*

"I'm sorry dear, what was your name," asked Agent Shamhat.

"Jan Siduri," responded the girl.

"Nice to meet you Jan, my name is Kristen. I work with the FBI and we are investigating what went on here. Do you have any other information that might help us?"

Jan thought for a minute before responding. "The only other thing I can think of is asking her boyfriend and his brother. They live across the street in that apartment building."

"Do you know their names?"

"Gabriel and Alex. Gabriel is the older brother. I thought I would have seen them out here, but they never came outside. I sent a text to Alex but he hasn't responded yet. Maybe they aren't home."

Agent Shamhat was taken by complete surprise. *Gabriel and Alex, why in the world would those two be here. This looks more like the work of Uriel or Raphael,* she thought.

"Jan, this is very important, you said their names were Gabriel and Alex right?"

Jan nodded. "Yea, their last name was Mason."

Agent Shamhat was now ready to make herself known to the local police and to take control of the investigation. She felt that she had all of the information that she needed in order to begin drawing a conclusion to the conflict that had happened here.

"Jan, can you follow me please, I will have some more questions for you," said Agent Shamhat lifting the yellow police line tape and directing Jan underneath of it.

Sheriff Jon Faulk stood on the outskirts of the now decimated residence of Martin Bishop. His deputies had already searched the area with help from the local fire department but they haven't been able to find the bodies of the Bishops. Looking out toward the police tape, he saw a tall brunet woman in a black suit approaching with a young girl that the Sheriff knew was Cady Bishops' best friend. Sheriff Faulk guessed that this was the FBI agent that had been sent from the Los Angeles division. He had gotten word two hours ago that the agent was en-route. As the woman came within twenty feet of the Sheriff, several of his deputies stepped in front of her blocking her path. She woman removed her identification from her suit and showed it to the deputies and they let her pass.

"Sheriff Faulk, I'm Agent Shamhat, I'm sure you were notified of my arrival."

"Yes ma'am. Just call me Jon, we are a informal around here."

"Well Jon, what have we got?"

Sheriff Faulk looked at the girl beside Agent Shamhat with a look of sorrow before turning to the collapsed and burned structure that was once the Bishop residence.

"We were dispatched at one o'clock in the morning for an explosion and gunshots at this residence. When we arrived we found the residence burning and contacted the fire department. We recovered two bodies immediately; one was located in the secondary bedroom probably occupied by Bishop's daughter. The second was found across the street behind that apartment building," said the Sheriff pointing.

"What was the cause of death of the victims," asked agent Shamhat.

"The first body was burned pretty badly but we did find at least seven gunshot wounds from a 9mm. The second had his throat cut and died of exsanguination. We have photographed the bodies and they are currently en-route to the coroner's office. We did encounter some trouble identifying these men. Finger print analysis and dental records are inconclusive."

"May I see the victim's photos," asked Agent Shamhat.

Sheriff Faulk moved to his cruiser and removed the laptop from its placement near the dash. He pulled up several crime scene photos and cycled through them until the photos of the victims were located. Spinning the laptop so that Agent Shamhat could see them, she was awestruck at what she saw. She half expected to see the burned remains of Cady Bishop and the slit throat of her father but this was obviously not the case. She stared in confusion at two individuals that she had been tracking for the better part of two years.

"Well Sheriff, these are certainly not victims."

"Ma'am?"

"These men are professional assassins, some of the best in the world. The individual with 3rd degree burns is known as Raphael and the one with the knife wound is Danyel."

"How do you know so much about these men," asked Sheriff Faulk surprised.

"As I said Jon, I have been tracking this group for nearly two years. These men are more dangerous than you can imagine. Only a select few of them have ever been seen but every time that I close in on one of them, they up and disappear."

Sheriff Faulk looked fairly disturbed at what the Agent was telling him. Looking back at the screen, the burned individual only had half of his face intact, but apparently Agent Shamhat knew them all too well. Interestingly enough, he couldn't figure out why these two men were killed last night. *If they were as good as this woman says, then why are they dead*, he asked himself. Taking a moment to think to himself, Sheriff Faulk turned toward the crowd of on-lookers and walked several steps taking the new information in. After thirty seconds, the Sheriff turned back to Agent Shamhat.

"So if these men are such good killers, then who in the hell got the better of them?"

"Actually, it was Cady Bishop's alleged boyfriend that stopped these men," said Agent Shamhat looking to her left where Jan stood. "You see Sheriff, the man that was posing as Cady Bishop's boyfriend was actually Gabriel Mason. I know that doesn't mean much to you, but please know that he is quite literally the second most deadly man on the planet."

Sheriff Faulk's breath was knocked from his lungs. *Could the young man that I met the other night really be a dangerous criminal?*

"Impossible," began Sheriff Faulk. "I met that boy a few nights ago when he pummeled a local boy for trying to assault Ms. Bishop. I sized him up myself as no threat. He couldn't have been more than twenty years old."

"Wait, what did you say Sheriff? Gabriel defended the girl, that's impossible," said Agent Shamhat.

"No it isn't," came a voice to Agent Shamhat's left, she turned to see Jan perk up enough to reinforce the story that she was hearing. "Cady told me about that night. This boy that is obsessed with Cady tried to hit her and Gabriel stopped him."

"So it is true, Gabriel has fallen from grace," said Agent Shamhat.

"Excuse me," asked Sheriff Faulk.

"You see Sheriff, these assassins take orders from a group called The Choir…"

"Choir," broke in Sheriff Faulk. "What are they some kind of Church Group," he asked skeptically.

"Not exactly Sheriff. Have you ever heard of the Choir of Angels? This is the same concept. Every member of the Choir has a rank and an angelic name. Their ranks are based on skill and kills. Gabriel is a 1st class agent of the Choir or Arc-Angel, so was your burned friend here. The other was a 2nd class member."

"So how does one man even at this 1st class rank defeat the other two here," asked the Sheriff.

"These men died because they never saw Gabriel coming. Like I said, he is the second most dangerous assassin in the world. These men would have been no match for Gabriel. If Gabriel really has fallen from grace, then we need to find him before the rest of the Choir does. This man can blow open the whole case that I have been working on. Names, locations,

Gabriel knows it all. If you think of the military ranking system then Gabriel would be a high ranking General. He will be hard to find, and harder to capture, but Sheriff, I will need all the help I can get."

"You have the full support of me and my men, but I have one question for you Agent. Why if this man was such a good killer, and a high ranking official of this Choir group, would he have protected the girl instead of killing her?"

"It's simple really," said Agent Shamhat. "Gabriel is in love."

Chapter 26
Tech Savvy

Alex sat in the kitchen of their secluded safe house monitoring the news and police band radio. He knew that the local police would have been called to respond to the Bishop residence but he certainly did not expect to see a state wide bulletin on the local news asking for information leading to finding Martin and Cady Bishop. They made no allegations of kidnapping or searching for a suspect but it concerned him still to see Martin's face in the television.

Still paying attention to the news he continued working on secure cell phone lines so that their location couldn't be traced when making a call. It was a simple practice that Alex was familiar with, requiring an inhibitor chip to be installed near the SIM card of a phone. As he neared completion of the last cell phone, the news again caught his absolute attention.

Watching intently at the on-scene video of last night's attack at the Bishop residence, he recognized the face of the local Sheriff, Jon Faulk. It wasn't the Sheriff that caught his interest but the brunet woman dressed in a black suit. Standing 5'8" was the fair complected Agent Shamhat. *If the FBI is taking over the case so quickly then they must have information linking us to the crime*, he thought. Agent Shamhat has been the agent in charge of locating and arresting any members of the Choir. *Unfortunately for us, she knows Gabriel's face as well*, he thought.

Alex heard the front door open and close. Seconds later Cady Bishop walked into the kitchen and opened the refrigerator to find a suitable beverage. Alex noticed that she had not yet seen the news and made a snap decision to turn off the television before she could find out what was going on. When Cady finally emerged from the refrigerator with a Diet Pepsi in her hand, she quietly pulled out a chair and sat at the kitchen table beside Alex.

"Whatcha working on," asked Cady.

"I am making our cell phones untraceable," he said sliding Cady's phone to her.

She picked up the phone and sorted through her contacts and messages. Alex had subsequently erased the text messages that Jan had been sending her throughout last night and this morning. Cady appeared satisfied that her information was still saved the phone and placed it back on the table.

"So I am free to make phone calls?"

"No," said Alex. "You are free to call me or Gabriel, as well as your father on this phone. I don't want you contacting any of your friends. It's not that we don't trust you Cady, but it would be dangerous for them if anyone from the Choir found out that you were in contact with them."

"I understand," Cady said disappointed.

Alex pondered for a second what she and Gabriel had talked about as they were hanging the surveillance equipment around the perimeter but decided that it was not important. He continued working on Martin Bishop's cell phone but stopped himself short.

"Where is Gabriel?"

"He is finishing up with the cameras. If you would like, I can go get him for you."

"No that's alright," said Alex. "I need some fresh air anyway," he said as he stood up. "Cady, can you give your father back his phone and give him the instructions that I just gave you?"

Cady nodded in agreement taking her father's phone and left the kitchen.

Alex moved for the back door in the kitchen, leading outside. Standing on the old brown and splintering deck which stood about ten feet off the ground, he saw Gabriel installing what looked to be the last of the cameras. Moving down the rickety stairs and out into the back yard, he moved quickly toward Gabriel. As he approached he noticed that Gabriel was finished with the surveillance equipment.

"Gabe, I have some news about last night," announced Alex.

"Good news I hope," retorted Gabriel.

"Not really. The police are actively looking for Mr. Bishop. They have plastered his picture all over the television. It will be unsafe to let him go anywhere. That is not the main problem however."

"Oh," said Gabriel raising his eyebrow.

"Our old friend Agent Shamhat is investigating the crime scene as we speak," said Alex.

"So that means that the FBI knows that the Choir was behind last night's attack," concluded Gabriel.

"Seems that way."

"Be that as it may, I think that it's time to pay Agent Shamhat a little visit," said Gabriel with a smile.

"Oh come on man, do you remember what happened last time? You almost killed each other."

"That was a misunderstanding. I was trying to tell her to let her investigation into the Choir go and she took it as a threat."

"Gabe, it was a threat."

"Perhaps, but this time, we need her help," said Gabriel.

"What makes you think that she will be of any help?"

"I'm going to offer her my help in bringing down the Choir," said Gabriel with a smile.

Chapter 27
An Eventful Meeting

The next morning, Agent Shamhat walked into the 7-Eleven three blocks from the Bishop residence. Following a lead from Sheriff Faulk, she decided to follow up with James Sullivan, the boy who attempted to assault Cady Bishop a few nights ago. This boy may be her only lead in finding the Bishops and the man she had been tracking for over two years. She had made it her mission in life to track down members of The Choir and bring them to justice.

As Agent Shamhat took a few steps into the small convenience store, she immediately spotted James Sullivan waiting on a customer at the cash register. She decided to play it cool and blend in with the small crowd that was in the store. In her experience, walking into a place of business of a potential witness or suspect can shut them off because it makes it seem as though they had been tracked down. If Agent Shamhat were to get the information that she needed she would have to approach the boy as a customer; making it seem like a coincidence that she ran into him. *Of course, that doesn't always work,* she thought to herself. *But it's worth a try.*

She walked to a large stand of magazines where another young man stood perusing the latest Field and Stream issue. She picked up an older issue of Guns and Ammo and opened it to the first page. She paid no attention to the magazine but peered over the top of it to keep an eye on James Sullivan. Agent Shamhat knew that she had to wait until the store was empty or at least mostly empty before she could talk to the boy. If she struck up a conversation when he was still busy, there was a good chance of him brushing her off for the other customers. She really had no time to drag the boy down to the Sheriff's office for questioning so she had to do this right.

Looking around the rest of the store, many customers were just getting what they needed and checking out. Others were standing just outside of the store talking about what had happened last night at the Bishop residence. Agent Shamhat turned to pick up another magazine when she saw the same boy still fiddling with Field and Stream.

"Good article," she asked.

"Oh, the best," said the boy not looking up from his magazine.

Agent Shamhat now noticed that all of the customers except for the young man reading the magazine had exited the store. It was now time to make her move and she had to be as gentle with the subject matter as possible. With the history that James and Cady had he might think that he is under investigation. She put the magazine down and moved for the counter. As she walked she picked up some snacks to make herself look more like a customer. When she reached the counter, James looked up from his register and began scanning the items she had brought with her for checkout.

"Find everything you needed," asked James.

"Yes, thank you for asking."

When James was about halfway through with ringing up Agent Shamhat's snacks, she decided that it was time to ease into the questioning.

"Shame what happened to those people down the block, they seemed really nice," she said.

"Yea," was all that James said.

"Only working three blocks from where this mess happened must be an eye opener for you. I'll bet the young girl even stopped in her once in a while."

"I knew her a little better than that," he said.

"How so," asked Agent Shamhat.

"I wanted to date her for a while, but things didn't work out."

Agent Shamhat knew that she was onto something. She decided that it was time to reveal herself and question him more thoroughly. This could be a premature decision, but she figured that she had no time to waste. Every second that she toyed around with her questioning, it would be harder to find the Bishops.

"Your name is James Sullivan isn't it?"

"Yea, how did you…" James trailed off.

"My name is Kristen Shamhat, I'm a Special Agent with the FBI. Can I ask you some more questions Mr. Sullivan?"

"Uh, I guess so," said James.

James motioned for Agent Shamhat t follow him as he walked through the door way behind the counter leading to the manager's office. Another employee sat doing what looked like routine paperwork for a gas station. The man looked over his shoulder and got up from the chair.

"Can you cover my register for minute Dave," asked James.

The man walked out of the office without saying a word. James pulled out the office chair and sat down leaving Agent Shamhat to sit on an unpadded wooden chair in the corner.

"So what do you want to know," asked James.

"Well Mr. Sullivan, as you have probably guessed, I am investigating what went on in this town last night and Sheriff Faulk tells me that you saw Cady Bishop a few nights ago. I thought you might be able to shed some light on what went down."

"Three nights ago, I went over to Cady's house to ask her on a date. When I did, she called her boyfriend to beat me up. Nothing else to say really."

Agent Shamhat knew that the boy was lying, but decided to let it go. The real reason for the questioning was to get a positive ID on Gabriel anyway.

"James, what did her boyfriend look like," asked Agent Shamhat.

James thought for a minute before answering. "He was shorter than me, dark brown hair. That's all I could really see, it was dark."

"Anything else James? We need help finding this man. He is very dangerous."

"You think he had something to do with what happened last night," asked James."

"Yes I do, but we don't have much information on him. Is there anything else that you can think of?"

"No, sorry."

Agent Shamhat was no longer looking at James. When she looked around the small office she spotted large screen with a security feed on it. Peering into the screen she couldn't find the man who was supposed to be watching the register for James, nor could she see the young man that was reading the Field and Stream magazine. She stood up from her chair and drew her weapon. Although she was a female FBI Agent, she didn't like to be known for that fact. Part of her style was carrying a larger gun than most male agents. The gleaming nickel plated .45 caliber pistol was loaded and ready to tear apart anyone who drew down on her. James looked disturbed as she wheeled around to the door. Agent Shamhat turned to face him and silently motioned for him to stay put.

Agent Shamhat opened the door just enough to get a visual on the situation. She saw that the coast was clear and exited the tiny office. Walking down the short hall with her weapon raised, she could only guess that she was getting too close to finding Gabriel and that he had sent someone to stop her. She positioned her back to the wall and slowly stalked out of the hallway and behind the counter. She saw the man who had replaced James lying on the floor unconscious. Kneeling down to check for a pulse, she considered it a blessing to actually find that the man was not dead. Reaching for her cell phone, she flipped it open and began dialing an emergency number for backup but stopped short when she felt the cold, hard barrel of a pistol on the back of her head.

"Agent Shamhat, nice to make your acquaintance," said a calm voice.

"Gabriel," uttered Agent Shamhat nearly breathless.

"Not Gabriel, Agent, he is fallen; no longer a member of the Choir."

"Well at least tell me your name before you kill me. I deserve at least that much," she said trying to sound calm.

"My name is Jeremiel; it's a pleasure to make your acquaintance."

"I guess the pleasure is all yours," said Agent Shamhat.

Without hearing another word, the barrel of the gun pressed harder into her skull. *This is it,* she thought. She felt as if she would black out from the fear of having a gun pressed to her head, but it wouldn't matter too much longer anyway. She never imagined that these assassins would get the better of her, but somewhere along the line she made a mistake, one that would now cost her dearly.

As Jeremiel began to inch the trigger back, he saw movement out of the corner of his eye. Wheeling his weapon around to stop any would be attacker; he found himself also looking down the barrel of a gun, Gabriel's gun.

"Jeremi, you don't have to do this," said Gabriel.

"In fact I do Gabe; Marcus gave the order to finally silence this woman before she can expose us."

"You disobeyed him once, you can do it again," Gabriel said in an angered tone.

"I disobeyed because I owed you Gabriel, nothing more."

"By my count Jeremi, you still owe me one. Let the Agent go and we can call it even."

Jeremiel cracked a sly smile, one that Gabriel thought would signify his compliance, and he was proved right when Jeremiel lowered his weapon to his side.

"Ok Gabe, we are even," said Jeremiel.

Gabriel lowered his weapon as well and walked toward the counter. Agent Shamhat was now standing up and looking with pure hatred at the two of them. Jeremiel still had the same smile on his face, one that Gabriel knew well. He was obviously proud of something, perhaps the fact that he had now settled his debt with Gabriel.

Jeremiel now turned to Agent Shamhat and cracked a bigger smile. The female agent was not impressed. *Having a gun to your head can do that,* Gabriel thought.

"Don't be mad Agent, it was just business," said Jeremiel.

"Just business? I know its commonplace for you people to kill for business, but it's not just business to me asshole," screamed Agent Shamhat.

"Why so glum," began Jeremiel. "Gabriel just saved your life; if I were you I would be happy."

"Jeremi," interjected Gabriel. "I think it's time for Agent Shamhat and I to take our leave."

"I think your right," said Jeremi. "Things are getting a little heated around here."

Gabriel motioned for Agent Shamhat to follow him and she complied. He suspected that she was glad to follow him away from the man who almost took her life even if she didn't show it. As they walked for the door of the convenience store, Jeremi moved out from behind the counter.

"Gabe," yelled Jeremiel still in a calm tone. "By my count we are even, but I don't want to leave it like that so here is a little piece of information for you. Marcus has devoted everyone to finding you, and I mean everyone."

Stunned, Gabriel turned around and looked at Jeremiel. "Everyone," he asked.

Jeremiel seemed to know exactly what Gabriel was implying and nodded. "If they are not here already, they will be by tonight."

"Thanks Jeremi," said Gabriel.

"One other thing Gabriel; I appreciate all that you have done for me in that past, but now we are even. The next time we meet please understand that the outcome will be a little different than in the past."

Gabriel knew what Jeremiel was implying. They next time they met, one of them would die.

"Ok Jeremi, I'll see you later then."

"Later my friend."

Gabriel and Agent Shamhat walked out of the convenience store and got into his black Ford Escape. Agent Shamhat was completely silent as they pulled out of the parking lot and headed east. Gabriel thought it might be a little much for her to take in, but she was definitely glad to get as far from her would-be killer as possible.

Chapter 28
An Unlikely Ally

Gabriel drove for nearly twenty minutes before Agent Shamhat finally spoke. "What the hell happened back there?"

"Jeremi owed me one. I came here with a purpose and that was to save your life. I'm sure that you understand that you are still in danger though."

"I really didn't think that the Choir would be brave enough to take on the FBI," she said.

"Agent, they have no problem killing anyone who gets in their way and for someone like you, who knows several of our faces, would have been a mistake not to have you killed."

Gabriel briefed Agent Shamhat on the situation he had gotten himself into by not killing Cady Bishop, and then explained in detail what had happened last night. She was literally hanging on every word that Gabriel had to say. Every time Agent Shamhat began to ask a question Gabriel would continue with his story cutting her off. She was not used to someone being so open with her and she knew that these circumstances warranted his being open with her.

"How can I believe anything you say Gabriel. I still haven't forgotten what happened the last time that I caught up with you."

"Agent," he began.

"Kristen, just call me Kristen."

"Ok Kristen, two years ago when you found me, it was because I wanted you to find me. You seem like a good person, and I don't kill good people. It was merely a warning that you were becoming a thorn in the Choir's side."

"Some warning," she said remembering looking down the barrel of Gabriel's weapons as he threatened her. For several moments they were locked in a stand-off and Gabriel eventually won by showing her that he did not come alone. His partner, stationed on the building adjacent to where they stood had a laser sighted weapon trained on her.

"So why did you choose to save my life? What could possibly be in this for you," asked Kristen.

"I plan on bringing the Choir down and I need your help. I have access to their files, names locations, and the leader. Unfortunately for me, I will need all the help I can get since I have the entire membership gunning for me."

"What makes you think that I will help you Gabriel? You're a criminal and I'm an FBI agent."

"I know you will help me because your life hangs in the balance too. Not only will the Choir have me killed, but they will still be gunning for you as well. It's no secret to any member of the choir that you know some of us by name and face, and there have been many who wanted to take you out before. Now it appears as though they have the green light. Trust me, you can't run from these people. Eventually they will find you, and when they do, chances are you won't even see it coming."

Kristen seemed as though she was aware that Gabriel was telling the truth. If she knew half as much as Gabriel thinks she does, then he would have no problems with her. It still seemed like she was in a little bit of shock from her encounter with Jeremiel and Gabriel hoped that it would pass quickly. They continued their long drive toward the safe house. Gabriel was a little nervous about exposing their location to someone who wasn't totally onboard yet but this was a risk that he had to take. It was another twenty minutes before Agent Shamhat began to calm herself and relax a little. She looked around the vehicle cautiously as if seeing it for the first time. When she leaned back to look in the back seat, Gabriel thought that she was probably looking for a dead body, which made him smile.

"I don't keep dead bodies in my car if that's what you're looking for."

"Where do you keep them," asked Kristen, slightly disturbed.

"I dump them near daycare centers," he said with a laugh.

"Funny," was all Kristen said.

"Just trying to lighten the mood," retorted Gabriel.

"Gabriel, let's get down to brass tacks here. Before I agree to anything, I need to know what you plan to do to me."

"Agent, if I wanted you dead you would be already. I don't get pleasure from killing people. I could just as easily let Jeremiel do it for me. As I said before, I'm going after the Choir and I need your help. With my knowledge combined with yours we will have all the information that we need to bring them down."

"Why the change of loyalty," asked Kristen.

"There are several reasons really, but sending me for Cady was the straw that broke the camel's back. Not to mention trying to kill me."

"I still don't understand, you're an assassin, what do you have against killing people?"

"I don't kill anyone that doesn't deserve it. Everyone I have taken out in the past has done something to bring me there. Cady however, is targeted for the vengeance of a grieving father. A father that would still have a son if he weren't doing something illegal; I don't roll like that."

"Great, an assassin with a conscience," said Kristen.

"So fill me in Gabriel, I want to know names, faces and locations of all assassins on the payroll."

"All in due time agent, but I can say with absolute certainty, that the location of every member of the Choir is here. Jeremi wouldn't lie to me and when he says that HQ was cleared out and everyone was reassigned to finding me. That sort of thing hasn't happened since one of our other 1st class members went rogue before I was brought into the Choir."

"Who was that," asked Agent Shamhat.

"His name was Abbadon, and he was the best there was. To my knowledge, he was tracked and killed by a student of his, thus making

Michael the strongest and most respected member of the Choir."

"Abbadon sounds really familiar, but not through my investigation," began Agent Shamhat. "If your codenames are all angelic in nature, then who was Abbadon?"

"Abbadon has many names, but that was the most popular name for him in the Choir. You would know him as Lucifer."

"So he was killed by Michael. Interestingly enough, Michael is only a rumor in the FBI. There are many people at the bureau that think he doesn't exist. He is one of the assassins that we could never put a face to the name." said Kristen.

"Oh Michael exists. He is the one who brought me in and trained me. Besides the 1st class members of the Choir, no one has seen his face and lived to tell about it."

"I noticed that you were disturbed when Jeremiel said that everyone in the Choir was coming for you, did that mean Michael too?"

"Unfortunately yes," said Gabriel. "If Michael is here, then there is no hiding from him. He will find us; it's only a matter of time."

"Gabriel, why are you disturbed by one extra assassin looking for you? You are one of the best assassins in the world. I would be more worried about the dozen or so people already looking for you. What is so special about this one?"

"I was a little worried about the others but Michael is different. There could be a hundreds of assassins looking for me and I wouldn't be as worried as having Michael looking for me alone. With him out there, this changes my plan completely. You see Agent Shamhat, I may be one of the best but Michael is undisputedly number one. Alex and I are no match for Michael, he will kill us."

Chapter 29
Past and Present

Cady Bishop stood on the front porch of Gabriel's safe house waiting for him to return from his trip back to Shaver Lake. Cady had wished that she could have gone with Gabriel back to her hometown but she knew that he would have been against it. Although kind of resentful for not being able to join him on his trip she understood that there was just too much at stake to expose herself like that. Since Gabriel had left she had been watching the news for any sign of him, but nothing came across. She was more concerned about seeing something like *Suspect Apprehended* on the news, but she guessed that he was too good to get caught by local police.

Ten minutes later Cady heard the gravel crunching on the dirt road under the weight of a vehicle. Her heart jumped into her throat, hoping that is was Gabriel and not someone else. Finding the strength to move, she quickly opened the front door and went inside. She could see just as well out of the front window of the house as she could on the porch. As she peered out of the window, she saw Gabriel's black SUV pulling into the driveway. Ecstatic, she went for the front door, and in her excitement, tripped over the pile of shoes lying beside the door and fell. Picking herself up and quickly opening the door, she saw Gabriel getting out of the vehicle along with a slender woman dressed in a black suit. Alex had told her that Gabriel had gone to get help, but from the looks of this woman, she certainly wouldn't be much help.

Cady walked down the two stairs leading into the gravel driveway and met Gabriel with a hug. She could feel Gabriel chuckling as she held onto him and decided to break her embrace.

"What are you laughing at," asked Cady in a huff.

"It's as I you hadn't seen me in a month, I just went for a little drive."

"Well, you went back to where the police were looking for you. I'm just happy that you didn't get caught. Not to mention, I'm sure that the police aren't the only ones looking for you by now."

"Well you're right about that," said Gabriel as he turned to the tall woman to his left. "Cady Bishop, this is Agent Kristen Shamhat of the FBI."

Cady was completely taken by surprise. *Why would Gabriel bring an FBI agent to the safe house,* she asked herself. Cady quickly brushed off her surprise and reached out to shake hands with the agent.

"Nice to meet you Cady, you know there are a lot of people looking for you," said Agent Shamhat.

"Tell me about it," was Cady's response.

"Cady, before I agree to help Gabriel with anything I want to ask you some questions if you don't mind."

Cady looked apprehensive, but after an assuring glance from Gabriel she agreed. Gabriel motioned toward the house and began walking with Agent Shamhat following closely behind him. As they entered the house, Cady saw Alex watching the news and taking some sort of notes on a yellow legal pad. He finished as they entered the living room and stood up from his chair to greet Agent Shamhat. They shook hands and introduced themselves with Agent Shamhat taking the initiative of extending her hand first. After the apprehensive handshake, Alex turned the television off and sat back into his chair. Gabriel motioned for Agent Shamhat to sit and she did.

"Cady, would you mind getting your father for us," asked Gabriel.

Cady nodded and turned to run up the stairs, but found her father standing at the top beginning to descend towards her.

"Easy enough," said Cady with a smile.

When her father was seated on the couch beside her, Gabriel looked confident enough to begin.

"As most of you know, this is Agent Kristen Shamhat from the FBI. She is here to assist us in getting out of our little situation. Before she agrees to help us however, she has some questions for Cady and Martin. I filled her in on the entire situation starting a week ago and bringing her up to speed with everything that has happened since. I want everyone to know that Agent Shamhat is in the same boat that we are. The Choir has targeted her and her life is in just as much danger as any of us, so I believe that you can all place your trust in her as I have," said Gabriel.

Gabriel knew that Alex would be skeptical on involving Agent Shamhat, but at this point he didn't really care. They need all the help that they can get and with Michael out there looking for them it would only be a matter of time before he found them. It was a rough situation to put his partner in but Gabriel knew that without Agent Shamhat's help, they would stand absolutely no chance in the fight to come. Agent Shamhat looked eager to speak so Gabriel motioned for her to take the floor.

"Gabriel and I have met before, under different circumstances, she said shooting a sarcastic glare at him. This time I believe that we are on the same page. I would like to stress to all of you the danger you're in. I know that Gabriel and his partner both understand the stakes here, but Mr. Bishop; you and your daughter are in a world of trouble. I agree with Gabriel that police involvement is a slim chance at staying alive, but I think that the FBI has more than enough resources to keep Mr. Bishop and his daughter safe from the Choir long enough for Gabriel and I to bring them down."

Martin Bishop looked a little nervous about the entire situation and for good reason. It was not every day that one assassin comes looking for you let alone a group of them. He threw the idea around and decided to agree with Agent Shamhat.

"I for one am with Agent Shamhat on this. The FBI has considerable resources and can keep us safe. Gabriel, I appreciate all that you have done for us thus far but I think it's time for us to part ways. If what you say is true, and there are multiple assassins looking for us, then the best way to stay safe is to be surrounded by law enforcement agents."

Gabriel knew that Martin had a point, even if it was a weak one. He had thought about letting Cady and her father go with Agent Shamhat into protective custody but quickly dismissed it due to the Choir having already infiltrated the FBI many times.

"Mr. Bishop, I see your concern and I want you to know that it's your choice where you choose to go, however, I need to stress the danger that you will put yourself in by going into protective custody."

"How can we be safer with you than with an entire building full of FBI agents," asked Martin.

Gabriel decided to let Agent Shamhat's knowledge of the bureau speak for itself. He knew of several cases where his fellow members of the Choir ad been captured and wound up dead before they had a chance to be questioned.

"Martin, I know this is a tough decision for you, but I want you to hear what I have to say before you make your choice," said Gabriel now turning to Agent Shamhat. "Kristen, are you familiar with a man that was arrested about a year ago named Ramiel Dawson?"

Agent Shamhat thought for a moment then nodded yes.

"Ramiel was a third class member of the Choir. Named after the Angel of Thunder, Ramiel was tasked with killing a United States Senator. Obviously the FBI found Ramiel before he could complete his mission and arrested him. The FBI thought that this person was just a random angry citizen trying to get back at the senator for his support of the new harsher crimes code; this however was not the case. Ramiel was sent to kill the Senator for a previous indiscretion. A year beforehand, this US Senator was responsible for the unwarranted bombing of a Middle Eastern town so that his oil company could secure the rights to the land. Do you remember what happened to Ramiel once the FBI placed him in lockup?"

"Ramiel Dawson was arrested for what you said, but I find it hard to believe that he was an assassin of the Choir. Either way, he hanged himself in his holding cell."

"And did you find anything amiss on his autopsy report?"

"Yes," said Kristen. "We found traces of an unknown neurotoxin in his blood. It was written off as a suicide pill that he had ingested prior to his arrest."

"Well Agent, I can tell you that you are mistaken. You see, I was the one who sanctioned the hit on Ramiel and the individual that I was training at the time carried it out. I believe you remember who I am talking about since you just met him a few hours ago. If possible, Jeremiel will kill his targets with neurotoxin for a quick, painless death."

"It wasn't that quick," interjected Kristen. "It took three hours after his arrest for him to die."

"Maybe I wasn't clear on the quick part. The neurotoxin takes effect immediately. That means we were in FBI headquarters to carry it out. Four of your agents are on the payroll there, and I'm sure that Marcus still has some unnamed contacts there as well. There would be no way from preventing a hit on someone in your custody."

Agent Shamhat displayed a look of pure shock on her face. She couldn't believe that so many agents had been corrupted in the FBI. It did explain why the one named Ramiel died in their custody but it was still an impossible thing to believe.

"Kristen, I know this is hard for you to believe, but I am telling you the truth. If we were to put everyone into FBI custody they would be dead by the next morning. There really is no telling how deep the corruption goes. The only one that I knew I could trust was you," said Gabriel.

"So what do we do," asked Martin Bishop standing up from his chair.

"It's only a matter of time before they find us here. We will have to stay on the move until I figure out a way to get to Marcus while avoiding Michael. If Marcus falls then we will be able to bring down the rest of the Choir without a problem. Marcus makes himself out to be middle management, but I know for a fact that he is the leader of the Choir."

"Wait, Marcus," asked Alex.

"Hard to believe isn't it. The truth is, Marcus has been the leader since the fall of Abbadon. If you think about it Alex, Michael follows Marcus's orders. If Michael was sent to kill Abbadon, then he would have been next in line for leadership."

"But that would mean that Marcus outranked Michael at the time," said Alex.

"Exactly," said Gabriel nodding his head.

"So that means Marcus IS Abbadon?"

Gabriel showed Alex a coy smile as if he had just figured out the last piece of the puzzle. Gabriel knew that Michael never killed Abbadon but sided with him. Gabriel had figured out this little bit of information years ago but decided to keep it to himself. He knew that revealing Marcus's true identity would put the choir into upheaval and it probably would have gotten him killed to boot.

"So where do we go from here Gabe," asked Cady.

Gabriel had been thinking long and hard about their situation and finally came to the only conclusion that made sense. He had to recruit more people to help them bring the Choir down.

"Alex, Kristen and Martin, you will be moving toward New York from a southern direction. That means you will have t travel into Pennsylvania and go north from there. Cady and I will come directly east. I have a place to stop before we meet up in New York."

"Impossible," said Martin Bishop. "You will not separate me from my daughter."

"Martin, I know this is hard, but I want to make it very clear to you that if we are found, we will all die. If we split up, it will be easier to cover ground and make us harder to find. The reason that Cady is going with me is because she is the most high value target. The Choir may be looking for all of us, but Cady is the one worth money to them. They will put all of their resources into finding her first and I am the most skilled at avoiding these people. I know how they think, how they act, and most importantly, how they will strike. For that reason I will be the one to protect Cady.

Martin Bishop knew that Gabriel was right. Although he regretted it, he knew that the best course of action was to split up. Knowing that this may be the last time he would be able to spend with his daughter was too much for him to handle. His eyes began to water and his voice began to slip into a higher pitch as he moved toward Cady and embraced her with a strong hug.

"I'll miss you honey, but I want you to know that when this is over, we are going on a very long vacation. Just you and me sweetheart, just you and me."

Cady embraced her father with a tight hug. This hug meant more to Cady than anyone knew. It had been years since she and her father were not arguing, let alone hugging each other. Besides the obvious danger, Cady knew that she would be safer with Gabriel, and had actually been set on going with him even after this mess was over. Pulling away from her father's embrace she turned to address everyone.

"So when do we start," she asked trying to hide her excitement in accompanying Gabriel.

"Tomorrow morning," responded Gabriel.

"Gabriel, when your friend told you that everyone would be in Shaver Lake soon, what did he mean," asked Kristen.

"Everyone means everyone," responded Gabriel. "I'll let Alex fill you in on that."

Alex pulled out the legal pad that he had been taking notes in upon Kristen's arrival. He then moved to the television and clicked rewind on the VCR. Turning to Kristen, he decided to see just how many faces of the Choir that she recognized. Pushing play, the television lit up with the previous morning's news broadcast. Kristen could see that it was a report on the Bishops disappearance along with video of the house and the onlookers who stood outside of the police barrier.

"Kristen, did you spot any assassins at the Bishop residence when you were investigating the scene," asked Alex.

"No, but I wasn't looking for them. They wouldn't be crazy enough to show their faces at the scene of the crime with a heavy police presence."

"That's where you're wrong. The Choir has no respect for the police or the FBI for that matter. Look at the video and decide for yourself."

Kristen watched the first part of the news briefing and saw herself behind the police line talking to Sheriff Faulk. She squinted to see the onlookers who stepped in front of the camera, but saw nothing out of the ordinary until a small boy had shifted his position for a better look.

"Wait, pause there," she said in an excited tone.

Alex paused the video and looked at Gabriel with a smile.

"There, right there, that's Jeremiel," said Kristen pointing at the boy.

"And that's Uriel, Ariel, and Zophiel," said Alex pointing at the screen.

Kristen was shocked to see that the people that she had been tracking for two years had been standing right in the open yesterday and she didn't even know it.

Chapter 30
Michael

Walking into the briefing room of the Choir's headquarters, Michael was disappointed to be pulled off of his current mission to deal with an internal problem. He had not been told who the rogue agent was, but he knew the importance of silencing them before they could talk to the police. He had expected to find the briefing room full of assassins but he was the only one there. Taking a seat at the large oval table, he recounted his last briefing with Marcus. He was assigned to find a weapons dealer operating in Turkey who was selling his arms to anyone with an itchy trigger finger against the United States. Luckily, before being pulled off of his assignment he had already located the man. He usually liked to survey his target to find their habits and daily routines before making the hit but in this instance he had to expedite the kill. Once he received the level one priority message from Marcus informing him of the rogue agent, he immediately broke into his targets house and executed him, along with several of his bodyguards. It had been seven years since receiving a notice on a rogue member of the Choir and he knew not to take it lightly.

He sat for nearly ten minutes before Marcus entered the room with a stern look on his face. Michael hated to be kept waiting so as soon as

Marcus was seated at the head of the table he got down to business. Marcus slid five files to Michael, one of which was extremely thick, which Michael knew must be the rogue member.

Michael decided to open the smallest file first which had a photograph of a man he had seen on the news during his plane trip home. Martin Bishop was a prominent business man who owned a large computer chip manufacturer named Bishop Industries. The man had the number five beside his name which meant that he was only the last priority during his new mission. Opening the next file he noticed a tall woman with dark brown hair. He recognized the FBI agent immediately as Agent Kristen Shamhat. Chuckling to himself he knew that it wouldn't be long before someone was given the green light to kill this woman.

"Agent Shamhat has finally become too big of a problem huh," asked Michael.

"Agent Shamhat is fourth priority, but a priority none the less," was all that Marcus could bring himself to say until Michael had seen the other files.

Looking at the next file he saw a young girl with priority one attached to her file. The girl had brunette hair and bright green eyes. He continued reading to find that her death had been sanctioned by a Chinese General who had a beef with her father.

The next file he opened was thick but nowhere near the size of the last file. When he opened it he was amazed to see Alexander Brody's profile photograph. Reading down the lines he remembered that this was Gabriel's partner. He was astounded that this agent, a second class member of the Choir would be involved in this fiasco.

"Marcus, is Alexander still Gabriel's partner?"

"Unfortunately yes," said Marcus.

"Then that means the last file is…" Michael trailed off.

"Gabriel Mason, first class member of the Choir and currently the second best assassin in the world, next to you of course," said Marcus.

Michael opened the last file and sure enough found Gabriel was listed as priority two. Michael could feel hate and anger building in his heart. Years ago, Michael had brought Gabriel into the Choir and trained him. He quickly became one of the best and until Jeremiel was the youngest first class member. Michael could not find the words for what he was feeling.

"Marcus, are you sure that Gabriel has switched sides?"

"There is no doubt I'm afraid. During your flight home, we sent several members after him and only one of them is still alive and I have my own suspicions about that."

"What do you mean," asked Michael.

"Raphael, Jeremiel, and Danyel were the closest in location to Gabriel. I sent the three of them to ensure that Gabriel completed his mission due to his wavering loyalty in his reports. You can see the reports on the next page."

Michael looked through the file more thoroughly and found what Marcus was talking about. Reading down through the reports that Gabriel had filed, he could see a developing interest in his target, something that was common among assassins and their victims. Michael had certainly never pictured Gabriel as one who would defy the Choir for his target but here it was in black and white.

"You said that you sent three and only one is still alive?"

"Yes, as I said, I had sent Raphael, Jeremiel and Danyel to take out Gabriel's target then Gabriel himself. Unfortunately, Gabriel was lucky enough to kill both Raphael and Danyel. Jeremiel escaped with a laceration to the head from the butt of Gabriel's gun," reported Marcus.

"And you suspect Jeremiel of letting him escape? I think a more likely explanation is that Gabriel is better than you think he is," said Michael.

"Whatever the case, I want you leading a full team against Gabriel if our next operation fails. No doubt he will move again if he escapes but finding him won't be that hard," said Marcus.

"When will the next op take place," asked Michael.

"In about twenty minutes," reported Marcus with a heavy smile.

Chapter 31
Compromised

Gabriel sat on the sofa where the night before he suffered through a pain that he had never felt before. Just sitting there seemed to make the scar on his back flame up in anger. Cauterizing a wound wasn't really the most ideal way of treating it, but it was the fastest. He worked vigilantly on his laptop scanning the motion sensors and cameras. The forest wasn't the best place for motion detectors due to the fact that any wild animal would set them off but he was operating in the *better safe than sorry* frame of mind. It had been two full days since the Choir cut off his access to their databases but he had a way around that. Training Jeremiel was one of the more interesting points of his life. The young assassin was cocky enough to think that nobody would ever figure out his password so he never changed it. Gabriel entered his name in the access box and the password IAmDeath. Once he hit the enter key, the laptop began to flash and the databases began downloading updates to his system. Smiling, he knew that he could track the movement of the Choir's members and figure out their next move. With any luck, Gabriel and his party would be able to avoid confrontation until they reached HQ.

Alex was working on a new cell phone for Agent Shamhat so that she couldn't be tracked. Sitting at the kitchen table, he sat with Martin Bishop who had been silent since Gabriel's plan was put into action. *It will be hard for him to part with his daughter at a time like this, but it was necessary,* thought Gabriel as he turned his attention back to the laptop. Looking at the clock on his screen it read 9:37 PM. Gabriel cringed and decided to take a walk of the perimeter. He knew that the typical strikes from the Choir usually come between midnight and three o' clock in the morning. Standing up from the couch, the wound on his back flared up again and Gabriel reached back to try and massage the pain away but was too stiff to reach it. Deciding that checking the perimeter was a great deal more important than dealing with a little pain, he continued to walk toward the front door.

Alex took Gabriel's queue and stood up from the table and moved into the living room to cover the security cameras. Gabriel opened the front door and walked onto the porch where he spotted agent Shamhat standing to his left speaking into her cell phone. Gabriel looked at Agent Shamhat with compete surprise and she seemed to notice his facial expression telling the individual on the other end that she would call them back and hung up.

"Did Alex give you that phone," asked Gabriel.

"No, he took my other one, this is a scrambled phone issued by the FBI, and only someone with level six clearances can trace it."

"Kristen, those people working with the Choir that I mentioned, can you tell me their security clearances?"

"I think so," she answered.

"Ok, how about Agent Gerard?"

"Level three," she stated.

"John Mongo," Gabriel said back quickly.

"Level two, Gabriel don't worry, I'm not being traced."

"Jennifer Gregerson," said Gabriel as Agent Shamhat closed her mouth in surprise. "Well," Gabriel demanded.

"She's level six, newly promoted to deputy director."

Gabriel stared at Agent Shamhat in horror for a brief second. Quickly shaking it off he grabbed her cell phone and ripped out the battery. Grabbing Kristen by the arm, he lead her into the safe house and didn't let go until they reached Alex who was still sitting by the laptop monitoring the cameras.

"Alex, get Cady now, we have to move."

"What's going on Gabe," asked Alex.

"We are compromised. Kristen just led them right to us."

"Gabe, I have her cell phone right here."

"This was a backup phone that I thought was safe, I'm sorry," interjected Kristen.

Alex wasted no time, jumping up from the couch and running to the upstairs of the safe house. He knew that Cady was resting in the first bedroom on the left and burst through the door to see her nearly jump through the ceiling in fright.

"What's wrong," screamed Cady.

"We have to go now; the Choir knows where we are."

Without saying a word Cady hurried out of bed and down the stairs behind Alex. When they reached the living room, Gabriel was packing what weapons and equipment he could into his duffel bag. Alex ran to his side and checked the security feed which was still working.

"Gabe, slow down. If the Choir was here, these cameras would be toast; they would be the first thing that they would disable."

Gabriel knew that Alex was right. He tried to calm his nerves by going back to packing up their equipment but it did nothing to take his mind off of a potential attack. He continued to grab the weapons off of the windows that Alex had placed there during the previous night. As Gabriel moved back toward the laptop to check the cameras he spotted movement on the central camera in front of the house. He studied the camera for several seconds almost dismissing it as another wild animal, but looking more closely he saw the outline of a human approaching the safe house at a very slow pace as if to try and fool the motion detectors. Whatever the individual was doing to avoid detection was working because the motion detectors did not trip when he walked through their field of vision.

Gabriel quickly grabbed his weapon from the back holster on his jeans and moved to the front door. Alex and Agent Shamhat also took his queue and removed their weapons also. Each of them cocked the first round into their respective guns and stood at opposite corners of the living room. Martin and Cady Bishop took cover by lying in front of the sofa near the window. Gabriel looked again at the laptop sitting nearly ten feet away and noticed that the cameras were going down one by one. Each of the screens on the monitor was turning to snow as they were destroyed. Gabriel knew that they had little time to act so he decided it was time for a preemptive strike. Alex seemed to know what Gabriel was thinking by giving him a solid nod before making his way across the living room and into the kitchen. Agent Shamhat moved from the front door to the sofa where the Bishops were taking cover. She had decided that it would be best to have someone protecting them at all times. It would be no use for her to challenge an entire hit squad of the Choir when she had no idea how they would attack.

"Kristen, I'm going out there. Take care of the Bishops at all costs," said Gabriel.

Kristen nodded to Gabriel that she understood and pointed her weapon directly at the window. Gabriel took a small circular disk from his pocket and opened the front door slightly. He slid the disk out onto the deck and slammed the door quickly. He heard the loud pop of the disk and saw bright white flash from the window where Agent Shamhat was positioned. He opened the door once more and stepped out. As soon as he hit the front porch he spotted three assassins curled over blinded. He quickly dispatched them all with his silenced pistol. He moved for cover behind one of the posts holding up the roof of the porch and peeked around the narrow corners. He heard several loud shots and noticed that the bullets had whizzed past and struck the side of the house. Diving off of the porch he landed hard beside a tree that would give better cover. His back felt like it was literally on fire, but he had to push through the pain. Pulling himself up and making sure that none of his body was exposed from behind the tree, Gabriel peered around the tree for a better look at what was coming. He saw a small amount of movement on his right side and fired two shots in that direction hitting nothing.

Gabriel's advantage here is that the people who are attacking were not using silencers which meant that he could locate them much more easily that they could locate him. He figured if they are at least ten feet away then they would not be able to hear his weapon fire, which would be a huge factor in this fight. Concentrating on listening for any sounds that the would-be killers were making out in the forest he could make out at least five more assassins milling around in the dark.

One of the sounds seemed to be coming from behind him, which completely caught him off guard. Focusing himself on the new sound, Gabriel noticed Alex coming from the back of the house. Apparently he had run into some trouble back there due to the line of blood now flowing freely from his forehead and down over his left eye. Gabriel shot a few hand signals toward Alex the first meaning *are you ok?* And the second was a question to find out how many assassins that Alex could estimate were bearing down on them. Alex responded promptly with his hand signals telling Gabriel that he was fine but vision was blurred and that he detected five unwanted guests nearing their position. Gabriel nodded in agreement and gave another hand signal meaning *make your shots count.*

Seconds later Alex was huddled beside a fallen tree which was lying across the forest floor. The real benefit to this cover is that the tree was freshly fallen and still had leaves attached to it which camouflaged Alex from sight. Gabriel on the other hand, kneeling with his back against a large tree that was still standing was completely exposed. Gabriel heard a sound coming from his left and leaned his head out just far enough to see who was coming. This time he spotted a darkened individual dressed in all black pointing a weapon in his direction. The man fired two quick shots at Gabriel's exposed head but the bullets went wide and missed Gabriel by several feet. Gabriel wheeled his body around to face the individual and raised his weapon also firing two times striking the man in the chest and head. As the man fell, Gabriel jumped up from his covered position and rushed for another tree which would provide better coverage. As he rushed he threw a hand signal to Alex telling him of his movement. Alex took the signal and fired blindly into the night to cover his partner. Gabriel could hear the gunshots of several more assassins approaching his position but they were silenced as they took cover from Alex's fire.

Inside of the safe house, Cady could hear multiple gunshots as she and her father took cover at the base of the sofa. Agent Shamhat had her back pressed against the wall next to the front window and every few seconds would thrust her head out the window to check for any immediate danger. Holding her weapon with two hands near her hip she ducked down to the bottom of the sofa and reassured Cady that everything would be fine with a warm smile.

"Martin, do you know how to use one of these," asked Kristen as she handed him a compact pistol from her ankle holster.

Martin bishop nodded and accepted the gun cocking it as if to reassure Kristen that he was proficient with the weapon.

"I need you to keep that weapon pointed toward the kitchen, if anyone beside Gabriel or Alex comes through there you empty the entire clip into them, got it?"

Again, Martin nodded and pointed the weapon into the kitchen staying low to the floor. When Cady's father accepted the gun, she felt his movement and weight leave her. She realized that he was not cowering with her but was trying to shield her from any bullets that may be fired at her. She saw a new man in her father, one that actually cared about her. Rather than using meaningless words, her father took action and protected her, which meant much more to Cady than he could possibly know.

Agent Shamhat now moved back into position at the window but when she tried to glance out it exploded inward as if some unseen force had been thrown up against it. Agent Shamhat instinctively leapt back to avoid the flying glass and landed hard on her back nearly five feet away from where she stood. Covered in glass and bleeding from an unseen wound, she struggled to brush the glass out of her eyes and stand up but found that her right leg didn't cooperate with the rest of her body. Looking down, a large shard of glass was protruding from her thigh.

Cady took notice of the large piece of glass sticking out of Agent Shamhat's thigh and quickly crawled to where she lay immobilized.

"Kristen, are you ok," asked Cady.

"I'll be fine but I need you to help me stand," she said nearly breathless.

Cady took Agent Shamhat under her arm and helped her scramble to her feet. Once standing, Agent Shamhat hobbled back to the window and put her back to the wall once more. She could still hear gunfire, but much less now. She was worried about Gabriel and Alex, which surprised her since they were two of the men she had been tracking for so long. Peering out the window again, she spotted Alex still hidden behind the fallen tree. She caught a glimpse of movement behind Alex and took aim. He was obviously unaware of the threat and she didn't want to call out to him in case the man only had a general idea of where he was positioned. Looking down the sights of her Glock .45 caliber, she quickly homed in on the man shadowing Alex and opened fire. The man was taken of guard and fell only ten feet from where Alex was crouched. The shots obviously startled Alex as well because he turned and pointed his weapon at the man as he was falling. Kristen then saw a thankful and what she thought to be a cocky smile from Alex before he turned back to fire on another assassin.

Gabriel heard the shots from Agent Shamhat's weapon and turned to see a man fall dead behind Alex. *He's losing his touch*, thought Gabriel with a smile. He moved around to the left side of the tree so that Alex could cover him, then took off left and ran straight into where the men were firing from. Alex watched in amazement as Gabriel poured an entire clip into a man as he leapt over a downed tree and reloaded as he hit the ground rolling. In an instant he was up again and firing at the remaining two assassins who were so taken off guard that they had no time to turn and fire before Gabriel's shots tore into their bodies. Both men fell silently into the brush where they had been taking cover.

Alex stood up from his position and yelled at Gabriel.

"Show off!"

Gabriel blew fake smoke from the barrel of his gun and holstered it with a cock look on his face.

"Serves you right, having to be saved by the FBI," Gabriel yelled back with a laugh.

Alex began walking toward Gabriel to see who the shooters were, but before he covered a few feet, he heard shots ring out from inside the safe house. Alex shot Gabriel a look of horror as they both took off running for the front door. Gabriel had gained a great deal of ground on Alex and was now in the lead as they sprinted up the front stairs and into the house. Turning the right corner, they found Agent Shamhat holding Cady on the floor and Martin Bishop standing over the now dead attacker. A feeling of relief ran through Gabriel's body as he bent down to check on Cady.

"She's fine, just a little shaken up from the shots," said Kristen.

"What about you, we need to get that taken care of," Gabriel said pointing at Kristen's leg which still had a large piece of glass imbedded in it.

"I'll be fine for now, we need to get on the road," she retorted.

Gabriel nodded and collected the duffel bags that he had packed before the shootout. Alex collected Martin Bishop and they both helped Agent Shamhat back onto her feet. Standing one under each arm, they assisted Kristen out to the vehicle with Gabriel and Cady in the lead. Gabriel climbed into the driver's seat while Kristen was helped into the back of the SUV followed by Alex who intended to treat the wound while on the road. Martin Bishop jumped into the back seat of the vehicle and Cady finally got into the passenger's seat in the front. Gabriel turned the ignition and the SUV roared to life. Putting the vehicle in drive, Gabriel floored the accelerator and tore out of the driveway looking in the rearview mirror, silently saying goodbye to the safe house for good.

Chapter 32
The Failed Attempt

Marcus had been sitting at his desk watching the satellite feed that they had so conveniently tapped into from the FBI. He watched as Gabriel and Alex killed the entire hit squad that he had sent. He consoled himself in the fact that there were no first class members of his team in the battle, but this was still a huge loss on his part. It would take years to recruit and train the amount of people that Gabriel and Alex had disposed of tonight. Enraged, Marcus stood up from his desk and walked into the hall where he found Michael standing against the far wall with his arms crossed and looking at the floor. Marcus knew that Michael had expected the hit squad to fail from the look on his face.

"I told you that they would be no good against Gabriel," said Michael with a smirk.

"You almost seem happy that he succeeded," muttered Marcus.

"No, I'm not happy, this means that only I will be able to take him, and I don't look forward to killing him any more than you did losing a dozen men over the past two days."

Marcus shook his head and walked back into his office with Michael close behind him. Moving to the window, Marcus glared out over the city of New York.

"You know what this means Michael," asked Marcus.

"I know two things, first, I think that Gabriel will go dark and we won't be able to pick up his trail again until he wants to be found, and second, that he is coming for you."

"Do you really think that Gabriel would be stupid enough to assault headquarters? It would be a suicide mission, one that he can't expect to survive."

"Gabriel is not stupid, he is most likely aware that you are the true leader of the Choir and not the middle management that you make yourself out to be. I also think that he knows your true identity," stated Michael.

"Do you really think that he knows that I am the one they used to call Abbadon?"

"Not only does he know but I think he suspects even more than that."

"Meaning," asked Marcus.

"I think that he knows that you are his father."

Marcus looked at Michael questioningly. *It would be absurd to think that Gabriel knows that much about me,* thought Marcus.

"Impossible, he can't know…"

"He does know, and that will be your only weapon against him," said Michael.

"What kind of weapon are you speaking of Michael," asked Marcus.

"The same weapon that you used against me five years ago. When I found out that you were my father, I decided not to kill you that day, and Gabriel will do the same."

"You really think that Gabriel will fail in his attempt to kill me because I'm his father?"

"He will fail one way or the other," said Michael.

"Meaning?"

"Either he will not be able to kill you and will resubmit to the Choir, or…" Michael trailed off.

"Or what," asked Marcus.

"Or I will kill my little brother," said Michael.

Chapter 33
Staying on the Move

Gabriel had been driving for nearly two hours. They were closing in on Las Vegas, which in his idea was the perfect way to hid in plain sight. He had a plan to split the team up into two, that way if one group was found, the other group could still complete the mission. Focused on bringing the Choir down was one of Gabriel's top priorities now. Not only had they sent him on a mission that they knew he wouldn't complete, but they tried to kill him twice now, which angered him greatly. This time he was bringing the fight to them. Finding a suitable place to procure another vehicle would be easy enough in crowded Vegas, but parting with Alex would be hard for him. Since Gabriel had been made a first class member of the Choir he has had Alex at his side as his partner. Now operating alone would be that much harder.

Alex sat in the back of the SUV with Agent Kristen Shamhat who was in a good deal of pain from her leg wound. Luckily, when Alex removed the giant glass shard from her leg, it didn't sever an artery. Alex continued to put pressure on the wound that had been bleeding for the past two hours. Kristen was resting comfortably while Alex continued to treat her wound.

Martin Bishop sat in the back seat of the SUV, every so often checking behind him to see if Agent Shamhat and Alex were doing ok. He thought about the recent events, and realized that he and his daughter would not be alive if it wasn't for these two boys. *Ironic*, he thought, *the two men sent to kill my daughter turned out to be our saviors*. He closed his eyes and tried to rest, but every time Gabriel hit a bump in the road, his eyes shot wide open and he was alert to everything around him. He had watched a program in his office several weeks ago about Navy Seal training. They underwent no sleep for a week on end, and every time that they tried to sleep, the most subtle noise would wake them. He wondered if this were similar or if it was just the adrenaline running through his body.

Cady sat in the front passenger seat silently, obviously still shaken up from the attack. Gabriel had hoped that she would be able to rest from their last run in with the Choir but that was apparently not the case.

"Are you sure you're ok," asked Gabriel.

Cady simply shook her head yes. Gabriel suspected that she was flashing back to those stressful moments of the fight. Shockingly loud gun shots, blood, and the prospect of dying was a huge psychological factor to account for when in high stress situations. Gabriel sincerely hoped that she would recover much faster to prevent a breakdown, but his hopes looked as if they would be squashed.

"Gabe, did you recognize any of those men that you killed tonight," asked Cady in a hushed tone.

"Yes," said Gabriel. "Two of them I trained when they were low level agents. The others are just on the payroll as subcontractors."

"Subcontractors," asked Cady obviously confused at the meaning.

"They are hired by the Choir to complete jobs that we either don't want to deal with, or when they need backup. The operations department looks to have contracted just about every known assassin in the United States for this operation."

"What does that mean for us," asked Cady.

"It means that we have to go dark for a while. It will be too easy to find us with this many people looking for us at one time. I'm not necessarily worried about the amount of people that they sent after us, what worries me is that they called in Michael, who is quite literally the best at what he does."

"How can having dozens of assassins looking for us not worry you, and what is so special about this Michael?"

"I can avoid any regular home grown assassin in the world, but, Michael is different. He was trained by a man named Abbadon, who until five years ago was the best assassin in the world."

"What happened to this Abbadon," asked Cady.

"I'm not sure why he left the Choir, all that I know is that Michael was the most senior agent in the Choir and he took it upon himself to track and kill Abbadon. Michael really never talked about it, but I have a strong feeling that what little he spoke of it, he was trying to hide something."

"So it still doesn't tell me why you are so scared of Michael. From the looks of things, you can handle yourself pretty well in a fight. This guy can't stand a chance against you," said Cady.

Gabriel knew that Cady was grasping for hope, so he decided not to go into too much detail about Michael. Deciding to omit certain facts about their kills during his training, Gabriel thought for a moment how to weave the story to make it sound more politically correct but eventually frustrated himself to the point where he knew that no matter how much he sugar coated the truth, it would still sound bad.

"Michael is really one of a kind. Do you remember in your father's house when I mentioned that I was trained by Michael?"

"Yes," responded Cady.

"Lets just say that he didn't teach me everything that he knows. If Michael and I were to face off right now, I would stand absolutely no chance at beating him. Our only hope is to take out Marcus, who is the leader of the Choir. Without him, the whole group will fall apart."

"I thought you said that Michael was the next in line after Abbadon," retorted Cady.

"He was, but Abbadon simply changed his name to Marcus. He thinks that I'm blind and couldn't see who he really was, but for some reason, Michael couldn't kill him. For all intensive purposes, Abbadon did die when he fought Michael, and Marcus was born. I intend to find out why Michael refused to kill him, and if necessary, do the job myself."

Martin Bishop heard the whole story between Gabriel and Cady. He was disappointed that his daughter had to hear such stressful words but he could think of no better way to relate the information to her. Gabriel was doing a descent job at keeping her in the loupe, but unfortunately, he was a little blunt with his briefings. He thought back to his trip to China and how everything went drastically wrong with the operation. The CIA had promised him that he and Clay would be perfectly safe, but as usual, something went wrong. Now Clay was dead, and Martin Bishop had a painful reminder in the small of his back about how plans can and will go awry. Martin remembered every searing moment of the CIA's intrusion directly after he was shot in the back by David Tanaka.

Suddenly as if he were hit in the face with a ton of bricks, he remembered something that he had learned from his own personal security force. If you cut off the head of a snake, then the body will die. This was the principal that Gabriel was working off of by planning to kill Marcus, but he knew of an even better way to save his daughter.

"Gabriel, I just thought of how we can at least save my daughter from this hell," said Martin excitedly.

"What do you mean," asked Gabriel.

Martin could see that Gabriel was hanging on his every word. This plan, in effect could save the life of his daughter.

"What if we kill General Tanaka," asked Martin. "This man was the one responsible for putting a contract on my daughter. If he is taken out of the equation, then the Choir would have no reason to pursue her right?"

"You may have something there, but unfortunately, they would still be after her. The problem is, now that you both know of the Choir and how they operate, they will still be gunning for you. I will admit that it may take the heat off of her for a while, and she would drop in priority so it might be worth a shot. I have been working out a plan that involves a similar scenario if you're ready to hear it," stated Gabriel.

"I'm all ears," said Martin.

"As you said, General Tanaka was the one who assigned the contract to Cady, and they hired us to fulfill the contract. My fear is that if we let General Tanaka live then he would just hire someone else to do the job. Another factor is killing him to take the heat off of Cady for the moment. They would drop her priority level and only be actively searching for Alex and I, but eventually would pick her trail back up. I think our only plan of action is to kill both Marcus effectively bring down the Choir, and kill Tanaka at the same time."

Alex perked up at what had just been said and leaned over the back seat to lend his two cents.

"You're talking about simultaneous hits on both Marcus and the contractor? It's never been done. How can we possibly bring down the Choir in New York and hit another man all the way across the world. I agree than if Tanaka found out that the Choir was destroyed he would immediately contract someone else, but what you are talking about is impossible."

"Maybe not," said Gabriel with a smile.

Cady noticed his smile and it made her sick to her stomach that someone could be talking about killing another human being with such a smile, but she thought that she would indulge him and ask.

"What is the smile for?"

"He's smiling," asked Alex.

"Yea, is that bad," asked Cady in response.

"Really bad," said Alex.

"I don't understand," said Cady.

"When Gabe smiles, it means that he has a plan."

"So what," retorted Cady

"When Gabriel has a plan, it's usually extremely dangerous.

Chapter 34
Parting Ways

Gabriel pulled into a small parking lot on the outskirts of Las Vegas, Nevada. Once they reached the city, such a large group would be easy to find, that is why his plan included them briefly parting ways. He circled the small lot several times to make sure that nobody was surveying the area, and also that there was a suitable vehicle for them to procure. Gabriel finally pulled into a parking space next to a tan Chevy Trailblazer. *Perfect,* he thought. Tan was another inconspicuous color and would be hard for anyone watching for the vehicle to spot in traffic. Exiting the vehicle he walked to the back of his Ford Escape and opened the back hatch. Alex and Agent Shamhat were still there, but Agent Shamhat looked much better from the last time he had seen her. She was conscious and the bleeding had stopped in her leg which was a great sign. Alex handed Gabriel a lock picking device called a slimjim and jumped out to be his spotter. Alex wasn't the ideal candidate to spot for Gabriel here since his pants were covered in blood from trying to stop the bleeding in Agent Shamhat's leg, but he was the only one with any lookout skills so he was stuck.

Gabriel inserted the slimjim into the front window and quickly popped the lock. He removed the tool and opened the door. He moved quickly by sitting down in the seat and popping off the ignition switch which then displayed several wires. He clipped three wires and tied them together with each of their ends hanging loose. Next he took the live ignition wire and struck it against the other three causing the vehicle to start. Turning to Alex, he saw a smile on his partners face.

"New record," said Alex.

Gabriel simply laughed and got back out of the vehicle. He looked at Alex almost longingly. This would be the first time that these two men had been apart in the past three years. Since Gabriel and Alex had been with the circle, they trained together, ate together, drank together. It was almost as if Gabriel felt more of a brotherly love for his partner than a real brother. The two men moved to the back seat of Gabriel's vehicle and assisted Agent Shamhat out of the back. She was able to put weight on her leg now, which was a clear relief to Alex. Gabriel knew that in her previous condition she may slow them down, but it appeared that she would make a full recovery in a few days. Gabriel was also relieved as he would need all the assistance he could get when they entered the Choir's headquarters.

Next Martin Bishop and his daughter opened their respective doors and exited the vehicle. Martin had been distant from Cady since the death of her mother. Always working or making excuses not to be able to see his daughter. Martin now realized that he may have passed up his only chance to be with his daughter, and tears began to fall from his cheek. Cady was an emotional wreck, something that Gabriel had hoped to avoid with her, but he understood the situation that she was in. Cady and her father walked toward the end of the parking lot for some alone time as Alex spoke to Agent Shamhat in the back seat of the trailblazer. She was obviously mad at herself for being wounded during the fight and he appeared to be reassuring her that everything was fine. Gabriel was holding a small grudge against her for being stubborn enough to call her contacts in the FBI and be traced, but it was a mistake and an untrained individual may not be aware of how deep the Choir really goes for their information.

At the end of the parking lot, Cady stood with her father speaking of things that they had done together when she was younger. She was glad to be able to speak like this to her father. It seemed to calm her to remember the good times.

"Do you remember our trip to Disneyworld" asked her father.

"Of course dad, it was when we still had mom with us," she responded.

"I never said anything to you about this, but I want you to know that it is one of my most cherished memories. I love you honey."

"I love you too dad," said Cady as she fell into her father's arms sobbing.

Gabriel could see that Cady and her father were having one of those father-daughter moments and he was glad to see them reconciling their differences before it was too late. No matter how hard he tried it may prove impossible to complete this mission and get everyone out safely. Gabriel knew that parting with someone after a fight was a very bad thing, and having it on your mind in your next fight could mean the difference between life and death.

Alex got back out of the vehicle after attending to Agent Shamhat and approached Gabriel. He had something in his hand, which Gabriel had no idea what it could be. Alex reached out and handed Gabriel two passports which he had made.

"In case something happens, I want you to get yourselves out of the country. It will be harder to track you outside of the U.S." said Alex.

Gabriel reached out and took the passports opening them to find similar last names between he and Cady's identification. He smiled and looked back up at Alex.

"It won't be necessary. We are going to take Marcus down and the Choir will fall with him, but thanks."

"Be careful," said Alex as he turned and jumped back into their stolen SUV.

"You too," Gabriel said silently.

Cady and her father were walking back to the vehicles as Gabriel climbed back into the driver's seat of the Ford Escape. He saw Cady hug her father one last time before they parted ways. Cady crawled into the escape and Martin into the trailblazer. With sorrowful eyes, she watched as her father pulled away wondering if it was the last time that she would see him. Gabriel knew what she was feeling and tried to reassure her that everything would be fine.

"Don't worry, you will see him again," said Gabriel.

"I don't mean to be pessimistic, but I doubt it," responded Cady.

"Hey," said Gabriel leaning in to be closer to Cady. "I will have you back with your father, I promise."

"How can you promise such a thing," she asked.

"Because you have only known me for a week and yet you trust me with your life. Cady, I never break a promise. I will have you back with your father, you have my word."

Cady smiled a reassured smile as Gabriel threw the vehicle in drive and pulled out of the parking lot. In his mind, he had no idea how he would make that promise happen, he just knew in his heart that he had too.

Chapter 35
Vegas Baby!

Gabriel and Cady checked into a Las Vegas hotel called the Bellagio. Gabriel had stayed here once before last year for a hit on a business man who lived in a private residence in North Vegas. As they walked through the Casino on their way to their room, the blinking lights and loud rings from people hitting the slots surrounded them. This was the place where Gabriel felt at home. Not only would the Choir not expect him to be staying in Vegas, but they would certainly not expect them to be in a strip hotel. Trying to take in the sights while keeping a lookout for potential threats would definitely be hard here, but he and Cady would most certainly be able to blend into the crowd if trouble did strike.

"Should we really be in such a crowded place with so many people looking for us," Cady questioned.

"What better way to hide than right out in the open," said Gabriel with a big smile.

Cady felt reassured once again by the smiles that Gabriel would display when his is proud of himself. The truth is, for her, Gabriel was sanctuary. She only truly felt safe when she was by his side. Not only was he a trained killer, but one that had fallen in love with her. She could tell that he would do anything for her, and that to her, was the best way to express yourself. It was gratifying to have such a dedicated person at her side. She pictured herself as having her own secret service detail like the president but quickly dismissed the thought; this situation was too serious for her to be daydreaming now.

When they reached their room on the third floor, Gabriel slid the keycard into the slot and it clicked open. As they walked into one of the most beautiful rooms that Cady had ever seen, she noticed that Gabriel had procured a room with two twin beds. She smiled and threw her bag on the bed next to the window and crashed down on the soft mattress. Gabriel rummaged through his bag and pulled out a watch and threw it at Cady.

"Here, this watch has a tracker in it. If we get split up I will be able to find you."

Cady picked up the watch and fastened it around her wrist. She took in the functions of the watch but quickly realized that it was already set. She noticed a small red button on the side, but before she could ask what it was, Gabriel was beginning to fill her in.

"This watch will not only let me track you, but it has a panic button on it. If you push the button it will send an alarm to my watch and let me know where you are."

"Kind of redundant, didn't you say that you could track me with my cell phone," asked Cady.

"Trust me, the more trackers on you the better," Gabriel said with a smile. "Besides, you can think of this as a wedding present."

"What," Cady asked surprised.

Gabriel laughed again and opened his bag once more. This time he pulled out the passports that Alex had made for them. He tossed them onto the bed where she was sitting. She picked up the passports and opened both booklets at once. Her eyes went wide with confusion as she read the names.

"Frank and Margaret Houser," she said looking up at Gabriel.

"Alex's' attempt at humor. Probably a way of getting back at me if he gets killed."

"Does this mean that we are," Cady trailed off.

"No, not in real life. Although, I can have Alex make a marriage certificate if you want me to," said Gabriel with another big smile.

"Listen mister, you have a lot to answer for before I will even be your fake wife," said Cady jokingly.

"Well since I don't believe in divorce I guess you're stuck with me," laughed Gabriel.

"Well, I am going to take a shower. It's been two days and I feel disgusting," said Cady.

"Ok, I will get one when you finish," said Gabriel.

Cady got off of the bed and walked toward the bathroom. Closing the door behind her, she looked in the mirror and saw that her hair was knotted and she had dirt on her face. She turned toward the shower and turned on the hot water. Stepping out of her clothes, she entered the shower and stood in the hot water for several minutes. As she stood in the shower, several things raced through her mind. Surprisingly, she wasn't thinking about what had happened only hours before. A dozen men had just tried to kill her and everyone that she was with, but it no longer fazed her. She stood thinking about Gabriel and how much she wanted to spend time with him. She was confused as to who this boy really was, all that she knew was that she loved being around him. Flashing back to the night that Gabriel had revealed himself to be an assassin; she remembered the kiss that they shared. Their lips fit perfectly together. Granted that she really had no experience in kissing men, but there was something about Gabriel that she couldn't explain. Although he was sent to kill her, and almost went through with it according to him, she wasn't mad at all. *Of course, he doesn't have to know that,* she thought with a smile. *I still have to play hard to get.*

Sitting on the soft bed in their hotel room, Gabriel was thinking of Cady. He also flashed back to their first kiss. It was odd that with everything that had happened, he was only concerned with protecting her. He hadn't felt this way about anyone before, and it scared him. He tried to think of any excuse to talk more with her, but was more nervous than he had been on his first kill. *It's odd that I can kill a human being, yet still be scared to talk to the girl that I fell in love with.* Gabriel began to unpack his clothes from the suitcase and stuff them into the dresser that the Bellagio had provided. Leaving room for Cady's belongings, he only used the first two dressers. Still thinking of Cady, he was startled when he felt the vibration of his cell phone that was nestled in his pocket. Reaching for the untraceable phone, he looked at the caller ID and saw ALEX.

"Frank and Margaret," he answered.

"I thought you would like those names," laughed Alex. "Just wanted to check in; we rented a room at the Desert Lodge for the night. I need to care for Kristen's leg some more and can't do that from the road."

"Will that put you behind schedule," asked Gabriel.

"Not if we check out by seven," responded Alex.

"Good, I want to arrive in New York at the same time. I am going to send the details to your laptop tonight."

"Gotcha," said Alex. "When will you be leaving Vegas?"

"Three days," said Gabriel. "I booked Cady and I on a flight to JFK and we should arrive at the same time you do."

"Flying huh, ballzy. But I imagine that even Michael won't see that one coming," said Alex.

"He certainly won't. I want to avoid as much confrontation as possible, especially with him."

"Alright man, I have to run and take care of Kristen's leg. Let me know if anything else comes up."

"Will do," said Gabriel as he closed the phone.

His timing was perfect. Just as he had closed the cell phone, Cady stepped out of the bathroom in a white body-length towel. She walked over to her bag and pulled out a pink t-shirt and a pair of jeans.

"Shower is all yours," she said.

"Excellent. I'll only be a minute. Make sure you don't leave," he responded.

"Not going anywhere," she said with an exhausted look on her face.

Gabriel grabbed a pair of clean blue jeans and moved for the bathroom. As he closed the door, he thought of how beautiful Cady had looked in the towel. Typically he didn't care if a girl was dressed or not in front of him, but something was different about Cady. When she stepped out of the bathroom only wearing the towel, he heart jumped into his throat for a brief second. Trying not to think about her anymore, at least until he was cleaned up; he started the shower and jumped in.

Chapter 36
Medic

Agent Kristen Shamhat positioned herself on one of the two beds in the motel that Alex had rented for the night. She was completely exhausted and found the lumpy mattress in the Desert Lodge to be more comfortable than the SUV. With Alex in the bathroom preparing to treat her wound again, she wondered if she had made the right decision in accompanying the two assassins. She thought of the Bishops and confirmed her reasons for being in this situation. Thinking of how the small party of five would be able to bring down the most powerful organization of assassins in the world made her leg hurt even more. She tried to contemplate how deep the corruption stemmed in the FBI bout could come to no valid conclusions. When she made it back to the bureau, she would make it her personal mission to weed out all of the moles in her division and make sure that they paid the maximum price for what they had done.

She spotted Alex as he came out of the bathroom with a small medical bag. He was drawing up a viscous liquid into a syringe and for a moment began to panic at the thought of a known assassin injecting something into her, but the thought faded as pain shot up her leg once more. She looked at him with worry in her eyes and he seemed to understand what she was thinking. Holding up the syringe, he began to explain what he would be doing with the wound.

"It's a numbing agent, nothing more. It will let me stitch your leg without the pain," said Alex.

Kristen nodded her head and positioned her back against the headboard of the bed. She was sitting completely still, but the thought of Alex with a needle still worried her. She glanced over to see Martin Bishop on the other bed trying to relax, but she could see in his eyes that he was more worried about his daughter than sleep at the moment.

"She will be fine Mr. Bishop, I'm sure of it," said Kristen trying to make him feel more at ease.

"She will be fine," repeated Martin Bishop. "She is being protected by someone sent to kill her. She has an entire organization of assassins after her, as do we, and you think she will be fine."

"I have been tracking Gabriel and Alex here for several years. Trust me when I tell you that they are better than you think. These two boys have evaded the FBI since they killed a U.S. Senator two years ago. If Gabriel doesn't want to be found, then nobody will find him, it's as simple as that.

Alex continued to inject the numbing agent into Kristen's leg. The wound to him was minor and easily treatable, but he was trying to be careful so that she could be back at 100% by the time they reached New York. After the injection, he pulled out a small needle and stitching thread. He estimated that she would need between ten and fifteen stitches, so he cut off a length of thread to match. As he inserted the needle into her leg for the first time, he wanted to make sure that Kristen wasn't in any pain.

"Can you feel that," he asked.

"Only a little bit of pressure, no pain," she responded not trying to look at the wound.

Martin Bishop rolled off of the bed and came to Kristen's side. He put his hand in her shoulder as if to comfort her.

"I didn't mean to snap at you earlier, I'm just worried about my daughter."

"Its fine Mr. Bishop, I understand. Cady is your only daughter, and she means the world to you. Please don't think anything of it."

"Call me Martin, if you would," he said with a smile.

Alex was nearly finished with the stitching and he was grateful for Martin's help in keeping Kristen calm. He moved for his medical bag and pulled out a new syringe and some antibiotics to prevent infection. He drew up the antibiotic into the syringe and swabbed Kristen's arm with an alcohol prep. As hi injected the liquid into her arm, he saw Kristen wince in pain. *Funny, she's an FBI Agent, isn't afraid to kill someone, and just took a huge piece of glass to the leg, yet she's squeamish around needles,* Alex thought. When he finished, he looked up at Kristen who was now smiling a warm smile.

"All done," she asked.

"Yea, just need to bandage it for the night. You should get some sleep. I still have some work to do so I'll take the first watch."

Kristen nodded and closed her eyes. Although she was with this assassin and quite probably one of the most dangerous people in the world, she was oddly comforted by his bedside manner. It was as if he cared enough not to see someone suffer, which was a weird quality for someone like him. She drifted off to sleep from exhaustion in minutes, warm and comfortable in the bed.

Chapter 37
Questions Answered

Gabriel stepped out of the steaming shower. He stayed in long past his usual shower, but the hot water felt so good on his aching muscles. Soaking wet, he dried himself off as best as he could and slipped on the pair of jeans that he had brought into the bathroom. He looked into the mirror and examined the wound that he had received from the car bomb two nights ago. He was satisfied to see that Alex had done a good job with cauterizing the wound shut. It showed no signs of infection or swelling.

Cady sat on her bed, watching television. She had heard the shower stop and was hoping to ask Gabriel if they could get something to eat. She didn't realize that she was starving through the whole ordeal tonight, but since calming down her stomach let her know that it was time to eat. As Gabriel stepped out of the bathroom, she noticed that he was only wearing a pair of jeans. She took in the sight of the muscular assassin as the water droplets from his hair dropped onto his large frame. His hair was still wet, and with it, completely messy. As he looked at her with his glowing green eyes and a big smile, she couldn't help but think of how attractive he was. Gabriel leaned over to pick out a shirt from his bag and Cady caught a glimpse of his back. She noticed the wound that he had received the other night when he saved her life. She truly felt bad for him having to go through what he did, but was grateful for his help.

"Gabe, can we get something to eat?"

"Yea sure, you want room service," he asked.

"Well, I would actually like to go out and get something."

"I'm not so sure that would be a good idea," he responded.

"It's just that, this might be the last three days that we have to live, and I want to see as much as I can before…" she trailed off.

"Listen Cady, you are not going to die, there is no way that after all of this I would let anything happen to you. I understand what you mean by wanting to live it up though, so let's go out and get something."

Cady's face brightened as she hopped off of the bed and threw on her shoes. Gabriel thought for a minute that she was a little girl for as excited as she seemed. He smiled and put on his shirt. Cady walked into the bathroom to check her hair, and by the time she walked back out, Gabriel was standing in the middle of the room ready to go.

"Hurry, I'm starving," she said.

"Just one more thing," said Gabriel as he bent down into his bag once again.

He pulled out his Beretta 9mm with silencer attachment and tucked it into the back waistband of his jeans. Cady was slightly disappointed to see him holding his weapon like something might happen but she understood why.

Gabriel and Cady left their hotel room and walked slowly to the elevator enjoying each other's company. They took the elevator to the casino floor and found signs pointing to the Bellagio Cafe. Gabriel had visited the Buffet here on his last trip and found it to be one of the best places that he had ever eaten. Being that it was now just after one o'clock in the morning, they would have to use the cafe. In-between the conservatory and the botanical garden they found the small cafe and seated themselves at the first table they spotted. A well dressed waitress walked over to take their order and Cady didn't disappoint. She ordered the biggest hamburger that they made with a side of fries and Gabriel ordered the same. He was impressed that Cady ate the way she did. Most women that he had known would never eat in front of a man. Once they received their food, they both dug into their hamburgers with ravenous hunger. Gabriel had been trained to go for prolonged periods of time without eating, but once he smelled the plate that was delivered to him, his stomach went into overdrive.

"Gabe, can I ask you a weird question," asked Cady still chewing her food.

"Shoot," said Gabriel with a smile.

"You said that a guy named Michael killed your parents. Then you said that he is the one that trained you. Why didn't you try to kill him?"

"Michael was sent after my parents because they were extorting money from a company that they worked for. What they didn't know is that the Choir owned that company and once they found out that my parents were stealing money, they had them killed. I was mad at Michael for a long time, but eventually came to see his point of view. It's just a job, and they did something to bring his wrath. He took me under his wing and trained me himself, which is probably why I have survived this long. Michael was like a friend and a brother to me then. He didn't have to take me in and train me, with the contract on my parents; he could have just as easily killed me.

Cady pondered what had happened to Gabriel in the past. She was interested to know everything about him, but it was clear that some facts about his past were very painful and she didn't want to make him re-live them. *I know he would have only been nineteen years old at the time, but I wonder what he was like before he became an assassin. It stands to reason that he was a normal teenager, but something tells me that some part of him wanted the life that Michael offered him; otherwise he wouldn't have become what he is today.*

"Anything else you want to know," asked Gabriel.

"There is a lot that I want to know, but I don't want to bring up bad memories for you," said Cady.

"Ok," laughed Gabriel. "But anytime you want to know something about me, please, just ask. I will tell you anything you want to know."

Cady smiled at the thought of being able to learn more about Gabriel. She was particularly interested in his past, and decided that maybe it was time to find out some of his past after all.

"Well, there are a few things that I want to ask you. I have actually wanted to ask you for several days now, but didn't have the courage."

"I'll make you a deal," said Gabriel. "Let's ask each other five questions, any questions you want, and we will alternate."

"Ok," Cady said with a smile. "Can I go first?"

"Absolutely," said Gabriel.

Cady thought long and hard about the questions that she would ask, but now that she had the opportunity, she couldn't think of anything that she truly wanted to know. *Man, this is like writing a report for school and getting writers block,* she thought. Thinking for another moment helped immensely as the first question came to her.

"How many people have you killed?"

Gabriel's smile turned slightly sour as he thought about the answer. He knew that this question would eventually come up, but could never figure out how to respond.

"I have taken out eighty six high value targets since I was brought into the Circle. As for how many total people I have killed, it's really hard to say, many of them had bodyguards."

Cady was appalled at the number. She thought that the boy in front of her would have said a much lower number.

"Were any of them innocent," she asked.

"That's two questions," said Gabriel with his smile returning. "But no, none of them were innocent. Many of the people that I have killed in fact were violent criminals."

"Fine, your turn," she said.

Gabriel wasted no time with his question. It was something that had been burning in the back of his mind since he had saved Cady from that idiot James. "Back when I busted up that James character in your front yard. Was he ever really your boyfriend?"

"God no," Cady blurted. "James and I were friends in high school, and he wanted to date me since our freshman year, but I wasn't interested. I have never really dated anyone since my freshman year to begin with. I've had one boyfriend and we never so much as kissed."

Gabriel was unusually satisfied with that answer. He hated to think of Cady as the typical girl in high school that dated everyone in her class. He began thinking of his next question while she was finishing up with her hamburger.

"What kind of music and movies do you like," she asked.

"I'll really listen to any music except for Rap and that club stuff. As for movies, I have just about seen them all."

"Really, I didn't know that you were a movie buff," she said. "Being that I never really dated in high school, I have seen just about all of them too."

"A girl after my own heart," said Gabriel with a laugh. "Ok, my turn." Gabriel thought for a second and came up with another question that he had about her. "What is your most treasured experience?"

"Well, most of my treasured experiences are a pretty old. Anytime that I spent with my parents while my mother was still alive was really all that I had."

"What do you mean had," asked Gabriel.

"That's two questions," Cady said smiling as he had done to her only minutes ago.

"It's one question because you didn't fully answer me. I asked what your most treasured moment was in life. You have to expand on it more than you have."

"Well, it's embarrassing. If you must know though, my most treasured moment, at least the one that I remember the most clearly, was the night you and I kissed," said Cady blushing.

"Seriously," asked Gabriel. "I thought that whole night was a complete nightmare for you. You found out that I was an assassin and you were almost killed."

"Before all of that Gabe. I thought that I knew you then, granted that I was completely wrong, but it is literally the best time that I have had with anyone in such a long time. Of course, the almost dying part was bad, but while we stood together on the lookout, I was completely happy, even if it was just a short time."

Gabriel felt horrible. He flashed back to their embrace and the kiss that they shared. He then pictured the gun in his hand, that she probably still had no idea was there. *It's time to tell her about that,* he thought.

"Cady listen," he began. "There is something you need to know about that night that I haven't told you about."

"What do you mean," asked Cady.

"I told you nearly everything about that night; how I was supposed to kill you, specifically around eleven o'clock."

"Yea," Cady said worried. "But you decided not to and we went to the lookout together."

"Well, I never missed that appointment," he said cringing.

"I don't understa..." Cady trailed off as it hit her. Gabriel wasn't supposed to meet with the other assassin and kill her at eleven. He planned on doing it at the lookout all along.

"Yea," said Gabriel with a sad look on his face.

"So the reason that you took me to the lookout was to kill me," Cady asked outraged.

"Cady, that was my plan since you asked me out that afternoon. I kept checking my watch, wanting to get you alone before that time because it was my deadline. If I didn't kill you by that time, then Raphael was supposed to kill me. But that's not the way it worked out. I want you to know that I had every intention of killing you that night. I had been on the fence about it, but I felt like I had to protect Alex since he would have been targeted too. It was when we reached the lookout, and I saw how beautiful you looked, how happy you were...Then there was the kiss. I couldn't bring myself to do it. Cady, when we kissed, I literally had the gun in my hand. I am so sorry for what I have done to you, and even more sorry that I didn't have the balls to tell you before."

"Wow," was all that Cady could bring herself to say.

"I know, I am truly the worst person on the face of this planet. I almost killed the girl that I fell in love with and it will haunt me for the rest of my life, however long that may be."

"I can't believe that you were going to kill me on the lookout. Alex told me that you had decided to protect me much earlier than that. Little did I know you had a gun pointing at me while we kissed. That is truly horrible Gabriel."

"I know," he said.

"I honestly don't know what to say. It's as if every time that I start trusting you again that you reveal some monstrous act that you committed and make me hate what you are. I don't want to talk anymore Gabe, no more questions."

"Sorry," was all that Gabriel could come up with.

"Well sorry doesn't cut it Gabe. You are a monster and I don't want to see you right now."

"As you wish," said Gabriel.

Without another word, Gabriel stood up and pulled out his wallet slapping money down for the check and walked out of the restaurant. He was sure that he had just sealed his fate with Cady, but she had to know the truth. In his mind, she was the most pure thing in his life and he didn't want to taint her with what he was. He sulked through the Casino and to the elevator, stepping inside and pressing the button for the third floor.

Chapter 38
Forever

Cady walked through the casino for nearly thirty minutes taking in what Gabriel had just told her. She was completely taken by surprise at what was said in the restaurant. Walking past several slot machines, she saw couples sitting there hugging each other when they would see that they had won money. She longed to have someone in her life that could share the experiences that regular couples do, but Gabriel would never be a regular person. They were currently fighting for their lives, and in hiding; what regular couples do that? She thought about the night that they kissed and for the life of her could not figure out why he would have told her that he was just second away from killing her. It was as if she was fine with the fact that he was an assassin, but knowing that she would have died in his arms was a lot to take in, especially now. This was the first time since he had revealed who he was that he wasn't at her side protecting her, and she felt like a part of herself was missing. Sure he had traveled back to Shaver Lake to save Kristen, but then she knew that he would be back. For a second she had to wonder if he would be gone from the hotel room when she got there. She pictured finding a note, or just an empty room, something that she couldn't bear.

As she closed in on the elevator, she thought about what she was feeling now and how she had felt when he had told her the entire truth. To her surprise, she still wasn't mad at him, not really. Sure, the truth hurt, but it was something that she could live with as long as Gabriel was at her side. She flashed back to the kiss several times in her head, and every time, she remembered the feeling of belonging, the feeling that she had someone who cared about her, someone that she loved. Then she flashed back to every time that she thought that she was angry with him for what he had done in the past along with what he still might do. She was terrified that he might still go through with pulling the trigger of his gun with her standing in front of the barrel. It was then that everything came into focus. She didn't care if he was sent to kill her. She didn't care if he still might do it. She didn't even care that she might die tomorrow. She knew that it was time to live for the moment. Thinking of what it would be like without having him around was too painful. At this point she couldn't even think of what a normal life would be without knowing him. She knew then that she would trade her life just to kiss him one more time.

Love comes in many forms, but what Cady felt for Gabriel in that instant could have been nothing but true love. He risked his life to save her, and since it had all happened, she knew that she felt something for him but couldn't figure out what it was. It was confirmed that she was desperately in love with Gabriel and she wanted nothing more to be in his arms. She knew that even with everything that Gabriel had said tonight, that he wouldn't have left her if he didn't think that she was safe, and even now she longed for him to be beside her. Looking back on everything that she knew about him, she knew in her heart that he was the man she wanted to be with.

As she reached the elevator, she saw that Gabriel was still nowhere in sight. She half expected him to come back to her and act as her guardian once more, but he never did. Pushing the button on the elevator, she waited for it to descend. Still, the elevator couldn't come fast enough. She wanted to imagine that Gabriel would be inside of it or at least in the room when she got there. She also thought of the emptiness that she felt and the sorrow that she would feel when she found out that he was gone. When the elevator arrived it was empty and her fears were all but confirmed. The last place that she would be able to find him was in the hotel room. She feared not for her life, but for her heart that he wouldn't be there either. As the elevator made its way up to the third floor her heart pounded in her chest. She felt as if the anxiety would over take her before she even got there. Finding that he was gone for good would kill her even before the Choir found her. Tears began to well up in her eyes, and her heart pounded faster still as the elevator doors opened.

As the large metal doors slid open, there stood Gabriel looking into her eyes. The tears still came, but Cady knew that they were tears of joy. She was thankful to see the assassin that had saved her life so many times before. She was thankful to see that he would still be there, protecting her. As the doors fully opened, she fell out of the elevator and into his arms. His hard body met hers as she sank deep into his chest. She hugged him so tightly that she thought she could crush even the strongest person. Nestling her face into his neck she began to cry happily never wanting to let go. They stood in the hall, embracing each other for what seemed like an eternity. Cady was still clutching his black leather jacket as he began to pull away.

Looking deep into his glowing green eyes, she could see a tear form and begin to fall from his face. She knew in her heart that it wasn't a tear of sorrow, but one of the happiness that they both shared in this moment.

"I'm sorry," said Gabriel.

"Shhh," said Cady, placing her index finger on his lips.

Leaning in, she removed her finger and replaced it with her lips. Gabriel pulled her tightly into his body as they embraced once more. They kissed for what seemed like hours, but Cady knew that it was only a few minutes at best. They were frozen in time together in a loving embrace, one that Cady never wanted to leave. Finally, the two broke apart and placed their foreheads together, still staring into each other's eyes. Cady was the first to pull away this time, leading him by the hand back to their room.

Once they were through the door of their hotel room, it was as if what they had experienced in the hallway repeated itself. Cady latched on to Gabriel and he held her no matter how hard she tightened her embrace. Heaven for her was in this moment, where she was finally able to express her feelings to the man that she knew she loved. She was completely happy in this moment, knowing that his feelings for her were just as strong.

"Cady," began Gabriel as he continued holding her. "I love you."

Cady's world was somehow complete hearing those words. Before, when they admitted that they had feeling for each other was nothing compared to hearing those words come out of his mouth. She had once told him that she thought she was in love with him, but now she knew that it was time to tell him for sure.

"I love you too Gabriel. I love you so much," she said as another tear fell from her face.

This time, Gabriel caught the tear with his thumb, wiping it away as he held her head close to his. This time it was Gabriel that leaned in and placed his lips on hers. The moment that their lips touched, a smile of happiness broke out across their faces. Cady pulled away from the kiss faster than their last, but this time placed her hand on his chest, feeling his heartbeat. She held her hand there for several seconds, feeling the rush of his heart compared to hers. Moving her other hand around his body, she began to force Gabriel's leather jacket off of his body. He gave no resistance as they stayed close, still looking into each other's eyes. Once his jacket hit the floor, she grabbed his black t-shirt and quickly pulled it up over his head. As he stood in front of her, bare chest exposed, she leaded in once more, and placed her ear to his chest, this time listing to his heart. Moving away, Cady grabbed the bottom of her pink t-shirt and pulled it off exposing her white bra. Gabriel's eyes widened, but before he could say a word, Cady intertwined her lips with his. With each kiss her hands caressed his naked torso feeling every muscle as if memorizing it like a map. Cady then moved her hands to Gabriel's jeans and unbuttoned them, sliding down the zipper. Gabriel pulled away slightly at the feeling of his pants being unbuttoned and looked deep into Cady's eyes once more.

"You sure," he asked.

With a reassuring smile, Cady moved close again and took Gabriel's hands, placing them on the button to her jeans. Without another word, Gabriel removed her pants. For a moment, they stood in the hotel room taking in the sight of their bodies before latching onto each other once more and falling into the bed. As Gabriel climbed on top of her, she moved to position herself to accept him. Before going any further, she placed her hand on his chest and looked deeply into his eyes.

"Tell me the truth Gabe; how long can this last. How long can we really be together?"

"Forever," was the last thing that Gabriel said that night, as their bodies became one and they shared every ounce of love that they had to give.

Chapter 39
The One

Resting comfortably in bed, Cady found that she had slept the entire night with her head resting on Gabriel's bare chest. A large smile crossed her face as she remembered what transpired the night before. The whole day was a nightmare, but her fairytale ending came at night. She was with the man she loved and she couldn't ask for more than that. Looking at the alarm clock on the night stand across from her, she noticed that t was already noon. They had both been tired, and after last night, needed as much rest as they could get. She tried to lay as still as possible so that she didn't wake Gabriel, but it was as if he was already awake.

"Afternoon sleepyhead," said Gabriel quietly.

"How long have you been awake," asked Cady in a surprised tone.

"Since nine," he responded.

Cady sat up in the bed pulling the sheets with her to cover her chest. She looked around the room and saw the noon day sun streaming through the window. Everything seemed much more beautiful after spending the night with Gabriel.

"Why didn't you wake me Gabe, I could have gotten up with you," she said.

"I didn't want to wake you. Besides, I enjoyed having you sleep on me. Definitely something that I could do every day," said Gabriel with a warm smile.

"Well if you're lucky then you just may get your wish," said Cady.

Gabriel got out of bed wrapping a light sheet around himself and walked into the bathroom. Cady sat with her back against the headboard and a big smile on her face. She thought again of the previous night and how much she loved Gabriel. It amazed her that she had been such a coward around Gabriel for fear that he didn't love her. *One minute I'm afraid that I will never see him again and the next I'm in his arms and he tells me that he loves me*, she thought happily. Getting out of bed, Cady slipped her underwear on and the pink t-shirt from last night and picked up a room service menu from the desk in front of her. Being that this would be the only full day that they would have in Las Vegas together, she wanted to make the day special for the two of them, especially since they would have fight of their lives come tomorrow. Today however, she wasn't thinking of death, the Choir, or the ridiculous amount of assassins that were looking for them. Today was about the two of them being together and sharing their love.

Cady heard the shower turn on and another smile crossed her face as she thought of Gabriel. *Is it silly that I am all smiles when I think of him;* she thought to herself but quickly dismissed it. Picking up the phone Cady ordered lunch for the two of them to enjoy in the room, then it was up to Gabriel to see what they would do for the rest of the day. A loud beep sounded from the night stand which made Cady jump. She turned around to see that the noise came from Gabriel's cell phone. Picking up the phone, she saw that he had received a message from Alex. Upon further examination of the text messages, Cady had noticed that Gabriel had missed eighteen text messages from Alex. With a small giggle, she opened the messages one by one to give Gabriel the messages. The first message came around 2 A.M.

I thought you were going to send the plans to my laptop.

Cady knew that Gabriel had work to do, but found it comforting that he had dropped everything to be with her. Looking at the subsequent messages, she found that Alex was getting both angry and worried.

Are you guys ok?
Where the hell are you?

Laughing as she came to the last of the messages, she closed the phone and went to the bathroom door. As she approached, the water stopped and she could see steam coming from the door which was open a crack. She knocked on the door, and Gabriel answered soaking wet with a towel around his waist. His warm smile meant that she wasn't intruding.

"I ordered some lunch for us," she said.

"Awesome, I'm starving."

Gabriel stepped out of the bathroom and began to put on the same clothes that he wore last night. Cady found it extremely attractive that Gabriel was putting on clothes while soaking wet so that they contoured around his muscular frame. As Gabriel stepped into his shoes, he glanced at Cady who was still standing in the middle of the room in her underwear and t-shirt.

"Do you dress like that for every man that comes along," he said jokingly.

"Only the ones that I'm completely in love with," he responded with a smile.

A knock at the door broke the concentration that they had on each other. Gabriel instinctive grabbed his gun from his waistband and moved quickly to the door. Before he reached for the handle, Cady reached out and grabbed his arm.

"I ordered room service, remember?"

"Can't be too careful," said Gabriel with a sly smile. "Besides, I would have to shoot room service if they get you see you dressed like that."

They shared a laugh and Cady moved away from the door. Gabriel reached for the door again and opened it far enough for the chain to catch on the lock before peering out.

"Room service sir," said a portly woman dressed in a Bellagio uniform.

Gabriel smiled and opened the door so that the woman could enter. She pulled a small trolley into the room and uncovered the two dishes that Cady had ordered. Gabriel looked down to see two steaming hot cheeseburgers on the plate.

"Classy," he said as he turned to her.

"Hey, yesterday was only the second time that I have seen you eat, give me a break."

Gabriel gave the woman a tip and instructed her to put the check on his room bill. After she left the room, Gabriel and Cady shared another kiss before digging into their lunch.

Chapter 40
Colorado

Alex, Kristen and Martin Bishop had been on the road since seven o'clock in the morning. Crossing the border of Utah and into Colorado, Alex noticed a significant change in scenery. From this point forward they would be on the road non-stop to New York. They had to make up for lost time, and that meant only stopping for gas. Alex wasn't particularly fond of being on the road for a full thirty-two hours, but it was imperative to meet Gabriel and Cady before they entered the Choir's headquarters.

Alex was worried about Gabriel. He had been trying to reach him since two in the morning and so far has received no response. Part of him wanted to turn the car around and head back to Vegas, but it would be completely useless since Alex had deactivated the tracers in their phones. Currently the only phone that could be used to locate them was Gabriel's. He had deactivated the GPS in the phones to make it impossible to find Gabriel if they were caught or killed. Alex decided at seven to trust his partner and continue with the mission. He did however, wonder what possible plan that Gabriel could come up with the take down the Marcus and the Choir.

Kristen was manning Alex's laptop for any sign of Gabriel's plan to begin the upload but so far she was coming up empty. It stood to reason that Gabriel may have just been too exhausted from the past few nights and fell asleep but it was nearly two in the afternoon. *He should have been awake and sent the file hours ago*, thought Alex. Never the less, Alex wouldn't let Kristen deactivate the laptop until he got word from Gabriel. The laptop was a liability on the road because it will send out GPS coordinated when downloading a file, but it couldn't be helped.

On the bright side, Kristen was ambulating much better than last night. Alex had figured that the stitch job that he did on her leg would suffice, but he never imagined that it would work so well. Without so much as one painkiller, she walked and moved as if nothing was wrong with her leg. Every so often he could see her wince from a little pain, but other than that, he was proud of the FBI agent for handling herself so well. Martin Bishop was asleep in the passenger seat, and only stirred when they hit an uneven surface on the road. He had been awake all night worrying about Cady, and as much as Alex tried he could not convince him to try and sleep. It was kind of nice for Alex to be able to speak with Kristen without Martin's constant interjections. Throughout the morning they spoke of Kristen's time at the FBI and more importantly to her, the time she spent tracking Gabriel and Alex. Two years ago, when Alex had realized that Gabriel was a little careless on a job and his face was caught on camera, Kristen got a little too close for comfort. Back then he knew that being arrested would have gotten him killed within several hours so they devised a plan to get Kristen off of the case. Gabriel had put out some false information that he would be in the Triton Building in Miami at midnight for a follow up job and Kristen fell for the trap. When she entered the building with a full contingent of FBI Agents, Gabriel managed to isolate her and bluff her into thinking that she had been targeted. During their brief encounter, Gabriel had convinced Kristen that she had gotten the attention of the Choir for the last time and advised her to stay away before slipping into the shadows and disappearing.

Alex considered it a blessing that Kristen was on their side, at least for now. He had a sneaking suspicion that she would try and arrest them if they made it through this ordeal, but Alex just laughed to himself thinking of how unlikely it would be for her to best the two of them. Continuing on their route, Alex tried to pass the time by making small talk with Kristen, but she was all business. He tried to focus on the scenery, but there were only so many mountains that one could see before getting bored. Noticing that it was time to stop for gas, he looked for signs to fuel the vehicle. Luckily enough, there was a rest stop only a mile up the road.

As they pulled into the crowded gas station, Martin Bishop awoke with a jolt. Looking around to get his bearings he quickly realized that everything that he had experienced wasn't a dream after all. Martin sat up in the vehicle without saying a word and stared out of the passenger window at the passing motorists. He dreamed of taking his daughter on a road trip like this, but thought that he may never get the chance.

Alex stepped out of the SUV and began fueling the vehicle. Kristen and Martin both walked into the convenience store and were lost from Alex's sight. He wasn't really worried about the Choir finding them here, but it was unsettling not to see either one of them for several minutes until they exited the store. Martin was carrying several bags of food and drink for Kristen as she tried to hide her injury. Kristen was the first to climb back into the vehicle, and without warning screamed for Alex making him jump, almost spilling the gas.

"Alex, message from Gabriel," she yelled out the window.

Part of him wanted to stop pumping for a minute and read the instructions, but he continued to fuel the SUV.

"What does it say," asked Alex.

Kristen read then re-read the message from Gabriel as if she didn't believe it the first time.

"This guy is crazy. There is no way this plan will work," screamed Kristen. "He is going to get us all killed!"

Alex stopped pumping and looked through the window at the laptop. Reading the message then looking back at Kristen he displayed a coy smile.

"This plan just might work," he said.

Chapter 41
Gambling and Betrayal

After Gabriel had sent his plan to Alex he knew that they would no longer be in contact with each other until they reached New York. This was the part that he hated, partners going dark and not being in contact. He trusted Alex with his life, and knew that those with him did as well. They had all spent so little time together, and most of them were together unwillingly, but in a time of crisis, every person can be made into an asset. The only real thing keeping Gabriel sane at the moment was Cady. After lunch, she had jumped in the shower and when she came out of the bathroom, she was dressed to kill. Wearing a simple pair of faded jeans and a white women's polo, Gabriel thought for a moment that he was in the presence of a real angel.

They had decided to spend their remaining time together having fun, so they left the hotel and began taking in the sights of Las Vegas. Their first stop was the fountains of the Bellagio, which was even more breathtaking in Cady's company. As they walked down the Vegas strip they found several Casinos that she had seen in the movies and wanted to visit. Gabriel had no problem obliging her and walking through some of the most spectacular works of architecture that he had ever seen. Cady was in love with the fake skyline of the Venetian so for dinner they sat underneath it taking in its majesty.

After dinner, they made their way back toward the Bellagio but decided to make a detour to see the lions at the MGM Grand. In the taxi, they didn't say much to each other. They held hands and looked at the bright lights of the Casino's. Gabriel had never been happier having her with him, even if the circumstances were grim. When they finally arrived at the MGM, Cady stepped out of the taxi and looked over the expansive hotel and casino while Gabriel paid the driver. As they stepped into the huge hotel, they quickly found the lion's den as it was a major attraction at the MGM. They were both in awe as they saw the humungous beasts playing with a large ball that the trainers had thrown in for them. One of the lion cubs tried to participate in the game that the lions played, but quickly found that he shouldn't try to play with the adults. Gabriel and Cady laughed together as they saw the lion cub being swatted by his parents. As they exited the enclosure, Gabriel could tell that Cady was tired from their day in Vegas. They exited the casino and hailed another cab. Once inside, Cady rested her head on Gabriel's shoulder for the entire ride back to the Bellagio. Gabriel loved being near Cady, so he slid closer to her so that she would be more comfortable. As they neared their destination, Cady lifter her head and looked at Gabriel questioningly.

"Gabe, this may sound stupid, but it's something I want to do here before we leave."

"Anything," said Gabriel with a warm smile.

"Can we gamble a little," she asked with a coy smile.

Gabriel's smile widened. "Well your passport does say that you are twenty one Marge."

Although Cady was initially mad at Alex for giving her such a ridiculous name for a twenty one year old, she was now grateful that she would be able to do something that she had wanted to do since she had seen the movie *Ocean's Eleven* and spend time with the man that she loved.

"Well Frank," she said laughing. "I will bet you that I win more than you at Blackjack in an hour."

"Oh," said Gabriel smiling. "What's the wager?"

"If I win, I want you to give me a back massage tonight, and not one of those wimpy thirty second back massages either."

"And if I win," asked Gabriel.

"If you win, you just might get some."

"No bet, been there done that." Gabriel said as he broke out laughing.

"You're terrible," she said.

"If I win, I want you do me a big favor. Any favor that I ask."

"What is the favor?"

"I don't know yet, but I want you to promise me that you will do it without question when the time comes."

"Alright, it's a bet," said Cady.

Gabriel and Cady sat at the first Blackjack table that they found in the Bellagio and went to war. They each threw down a hundred dollars and received their chips. Gabriel started out ahead but quickly lost most of his winnings. Cady on the other hand, was winning an insane amount of money. Within the hour she was up nearly five hundred dollars. With only one hand left it seemed as though Cady had won their bet. Gabriel on the other hand, was more involved with another man who sat at the table. Cady couldn't hear exactly what the two talked about but they were both in good spirits which made her happy.

"Looks like I win," said Cady triumphant.

"Not necessarily," said Gabriel with a sly smile.

"What do you mean Gabe, there is no way you can win more than me in the next hand. It's impossible.

The man sitting to Gabriel left looked at Cady with a bright smile, and folded his set of cards. Gabriel was only up two hundred and fifty dollars to Cady's five hundred. In his hand, he held a total of eleven and Cady had a seventeen. She waived her hand to signal that she would stay and the dealer moved on to Gabriel.

"Double down," he said.

Cady had no idea what that meant, but Gabriel looked sure of himself.

"You don't have the money to double down sir," said the dealer.

"I'll spot him," said the man to his left sliding two hundred and fifty dollars worth of chips to Gabriel's pile.

"That's awfully nice of you," said Cady to the man.

"Well, I owe him," said the man.

"I'm confused," said Cady with a questioning look on her face.

Gabriel turned to Cady with a stern look and tilted his eyes back to the man. Cady couldn't really tell what he was getting at and mirrored his glances at the man. The dealer flipped down a king to Gabriel giving him twenty one. The dealer then flipped her cards to read eighteen beating Cady and losing her stack of chips to the house.

The dealer awarded Gabriel five hundred dollars worth of chips and congratulated him. Cady was in awe that Gabriel had come from behind and beat her at the last moment, but she wasn't too worried about losing, only owing Gabriel a favor.

"So who is this man that has helped you cheat your way to getting out of my back massage," asked Cady.

"Cady," Gabriel began as he looked at the man. "I would like to introduce you to Michael."

Cady and Gabriel left the casino floor silently, followed by Michael. As they entered the elevator to return to their room, Cady had a terrified look on her face.

"Gabe, is this how it ends?"

"Not quite," interjected Michael.

Cady displayed a look of utter confusion as the elevator ascended to the third floor. Michael stood in the corner of the elevator with his hands in his pockets. She noticed that he was well dressed for the occasion of killing someone. Wearing black suit pants and a white button down shirt, the 6'3" man with black hair and brown eyes still stood with a smile. Cady glanced at Gabriel not knowing what to ask about the situation they were in. Gabriel was the first to exit the elevator and silently made his way to the room with Cady at his side and Michael following close behind. Gabriel slid his keycard into the lock and opened the door. He walked in and stopped in the middle of the floor directing Cady to sit on the bed.

As she sat down, all the fears that she had the previous night came rushing back into her mind. *IS Gabriel back with the Choir, is he going to kill me to satisfy Michael?* A million possibilities rushed through her head, but nothing could have prepared her for Gabriel's explanation.

"Cady, last night, when I left you in the restaurant, I returned to the room and called Michael. I'm the one who gave our position away so that we could finally end this."

"I don't understand," Cady said in a choked voice.

"Gabriel called me here to discuss your surrender to the Choir," said Michael with a smirk.

"Is that true," asked Cady as she shot another confused glare at Gabriel.

"Yes, I called to discuss the terms of our surrender."

"Gabriel, are you crazy? Our surrender means that we die. What kind of compromise is that?"

"Well Ms. Bishop. Actually only you die. Gabriel here will be forgiven when he delivers you to our boss and executes you in front of them."

On the verge of tears, Cady fell back onto the bed. She placed her hands over her eyes and tried to hold back the sorrow. She had been betrayed by the man she loved and nothing, not even death could be more painful than that.

"Cady," began Gabriel. "You need to understand..."

"Don't...Just don't Cady said with tears falling from her cheeks."

"It looks like you two have much to discuss. I'll be in the hall," said Michael.

As Michael exited the room, Cady fell back onto the bed crying. She had been betrayed by the man that she loved. Thinking of the night they shared, she couldn't believe that Gabriel would have done something like this. Gabriel stepped near the bed and Cady could sense that he was closing in on her but she no longer wanted anything to do with the assassin.

"Cady," he began.

"No Gabriel, I don't want to hear your excuses, just get out of here," she said cutting him off.

Gabriel looked as if he would throw up but followed Cady's order to leave. He opened the door and found Michael standing against the wall across from the room.

"Will she be a problem, asked Michael.

"No, her spirit is broken, she won't try to run. What about Marcus, I can't believe that he would let me come back so easily."

"Let me handle Marcus. After you killed so many of our own he was fuming but I managed to calm him down. Once you execute the girl all will be forgiven and we can get back to work."

"What about the other thing that I asked for?"

"It will be done, although I don't understand your request," said Michael questioningly.

"I just want all parties involved in the hit to see that I am back on your side so there will be no question of my loyalty."

"It's good to have you back brother," said Michael with a smile.

Chapter 42
The Choir of Angels

Cady had said nothing to Gabriel since he revealed that he was working with Michael to deliver her to the Choir and the man who had called the hit on her. The seven hour plane ride was the longest seven hours that she had ever experienced. During their trip, Cady looked out the window of the private jet that they had boarded hours before. The plane landed at a private section of the JFK Airport in New York. Cady felt like screaming for help to anyone who was standing near the plane when she exited but quickly found that the area had been completely deserted.

They entered a limousine and Gabriel sat beside her not saying a word. She could tell that he was torn over what he had done, but this betrayal was unforgivable. Cady had thought about resisting, but with Gabriel about to kill her, she had already resigned her life, not wanting to live without him. Even with his betrayal, she was consumed with love for the assassin who would take her life. Michael sat across from Gabriel enjoying a glass of scotch from the fully stocked bar in the limo. She never saw the smile fade from his face, something that was really getting on her nerves.

"So Gabriel that was some plan that you sent to Alex, ingenious really.

You are definitely the most underhanded person that I know. Luring Martin Bishop and the FBI Agent into HQ so that they could witness the death of the girl that they had failed to protect."

"I couldn't have done it without you Michael. This whole situation went out of control the night that I saved the girl from a beating by that stupid football player. This was the only way to get out of the state without having my face all over the news thanks to that damn sheriff."

Their conversation was cut short as the limousine pulled into an underground parking structure of a tall building. Cady could sense that this was the end of the line. She couldn't believe that her life would end like this. As they exited the vehicle, Gabriel was met by three people one of which Cady recognized at Jeremiel. The young boy had a wide smile on his face as he took Cady under the arm and began leading her toward the large metal doors of the elevator. Once onboard the elevator, it began ascending slowly. Gabriel looked around the elevator in triumph as he nodded to several of his assassin friends.

"Some trick you pulled Gabriel," said a tall woman with blond hair.

"Personally, I would have just killed everyone that got in my way," said the tall man to her left.

"Ariel, it's good to hear you admit that I am better than you," said Gabriel to the woman. "And Uriel, that is why I will always be better than you are. You try and kill your way out of the situations that you put yourself in while I use my head."

"Hmph," said Uriel crossing his arms.

When the elevator opened Cady could see a large empty room illuminated by a lone spotlight in the middle of it. As they crossed the expansive warehouse looking room, Cady could see that the concrete floor had a drain embedded into it every few feet. *This must be the place where they will kill me*, she thought. *The drains are for all of the blood.* Every ten feet or so, large marble pillars stretched from the floor to the ceiling. Jeremiel led Cady to the center of the floor where a large man in a black suit stood. Next to him was a short Chinese man that she could only conclude to be General Tanaka.

"Good to finally meet you," said the tall man. "My name is Marcus and the man next to me is General Ful Tanaka."

Cady turned sharply to stare at Gabriel. She looked at him with pure hatred and disgust.

"Is that all I am to you Gabriel, a contract," she screamed.

Jeremiel laughed as he let Cady go and she rushed at Gabriel balling her hands into fists. She was so enraged that she didn't notice that Gabriel made no move to protect himself. She slammed into him with all of her strength. She caught Gabriel on the cheek with a right hook knocking his head to the left. Ariel, the tall woman that Cady had the pleasure of an elevator ride with, grabbed her left arm before she could land another punch. She subdued Cady and held her arm at a painful angle until she settled down.

"Are you going to take that from her Gabriel? It's time to end this," spat Ariel.

"It will be done soon enough," said Marcus. "But first, I would like to introduce some more witnesses to her death."

Marcus held out a small remote control and pushed the singular button in the center. The room illuminated enough for Cady to see that her father and Agent Shamhat stood to her left. She could see that her father had been beaten and restrained. Agent Shamhat looked to be in worse condition with her leg bleeding from the wound she had sustained two days ago.

"Gabriel, it's time, said a voice that came from behind Cady.

Cady knew that the voice from behind her was Alex as he entered her sight. He walked to Gabriel handing him a silenced pistol, identical to the one that he had been carrying since the nightmare began. Gabriel took the gun from Alex and took several steps toward Cady before stopping.

"I know what you must think of me Cady, but I had no idea until I made the phone call to Michael that he and Marcus really are my family," he said in a choked tone.

"What do you mean Gabriel," said Cady in a harsh, unsettling voice.

"Michael told me everything. The people that he killed four years ago weren't my birth parents. Yes, my mother is dead, but Marcus is my father, and Michael is my brother."

"Lies," said Cady. "Don't you see that they are lying to you so that you will do this?"

"Think about it Cady. Remember the story of Abbadon. That is why Michael couldn't kill him. He's Michael's father...My father."

Strangely, it made complete sense to Cady. She understood what Gabriel was feeling. It was stupid of her to think that he could betray his family for a girl that he had just met.

"Cady, I'm sorry..." Gabriel said.

"Just get it over with," said Cady as she stood tall ready to accept her fate.

Gabriel closed the gap between he and Cady. Leaning in close to her, he whispered in her ear.

"I really do love you Cady, but you should have more trust in me than this," he said silently for only Cady to hear.

At that moment, Cady understood everything. Gabriel was still with her, this was his plan. Thinking back to him working on the laptop yesterday, she remembered him saying something about getting into the Choir's headquarters. Although she was frightened for her life, she could see the confidence in Gabriel's eyes. He had called Michael to bring them in, and got General Tanaka and Marcus in the same room with him.

"Gabe, before you do this. Can I have one last kiss," asked Cady.

"My god," spat Ariel from a distance.

"Of course," said Gabriel as he leaned in and embraced Cady for the last time. They kissed for only a few seconds before the deed would be done. Cherishing their final moments together, Gabriel and Cady held each other closely still locked together with their lips.

"NOW," Gabriel screamed as he broke away from Cady and spun toward Marcus.

In an instant, Kristen and Martin Bishop had pulled their hands free from their handcuffs and drew weapons from behind them. Uriel was the first to draw his weapon to defend himself and before he could pull the trigger, was gunned down by Kristen. He fell to the floor without a sound, lifeless. Firing erupted all around Cady. She ducked down to the ground before opening her eyes to see General Tanaka taken by surprise by Alex who emptied an entire clip of his gun into him. Marcus retreated toward the elevator along with Michael who was acting as a human shield. Gabriel fired several shots and caught Michael in both in the leg and lower back.

Gabriel had turned to fire at Ariel but she was too quick. She ducked behind a pillar that held up the structure. She returned fire immediately striking Agent Shamhat in the arm causing her to drop her weapon. Another shot came from behind Cady as her father had opened fire on Ariel. Again, Ariel was much too quick and avoided the shots. Gabriel grabbed Cady by the arm and pulled her to another pillar on the opposite side of the room. He placed her behind it and returned to the fight firing several shots in Ariel's direction.

Cady covered her ears but found that it was no help whatsoever. She cowered behind the pillar every few second poking her head out to make sure that Gabriel was not hurt. Gabriel was taking cover behind the body of Uriel, laying flat on the ground and shooting. Cady was sure that the fight would be over in a few more seconds. It wasn't until the elevator on the far wall opened and several more assassins poured out of it firing at Gabriel that she begin to panic once more.

"Alex," yelled Gabriel. "Flank!"

Alex understood immediately that Gabriel wanted him to fire on the new assassins that had joined the fight. Looking to his left he saw Kristen against the wall bleeding from the arm. Rushing to her side while firing at the assassins he picked up the weapon that she had dropped and tossed it back to her.

"You ok," Alex yelled.

"I'll be fine, take care of Martin," screamed Kristen over the sound of the gunfire.

Alex moved to help Martin Bishop who was pinned down but before he could take a step he was sent flying back into the wall where Kristen was positioned. Dazed, Alex looked up to see Jeremiel standing in the center of the floor smiling. Alex quickly raised his weapon and fired. Jeremiel took a bullet to the right arm moving his gun to the side as he fired back. Jeremiel's bullet went wide and hit Alex in the side. Before Alex could focus for another shot, Jeremiel had ducked behind another pillar for cover.

Gabriel fired several more shots at the assassins. They fell one by one to his accuracy, but it seemed like a never ending wave of assassin's replacing the ones that fell. Gabriel rushed at one of the assassins who had been hit several times. Before the man could hit the floor, Gabriel was rushing past him grabbing a grenade that the man had pulled from his vest. Pulling the pin and throwing it toward the line of assassins, he ducked behind the pillar before the explosion. The assassins kept firing on Gabriel's position not seeing the grenade rolling in their direction. Seconds later, the room erupted with a bright orange light and a deafening explosion.

Poking his head out from behind the pillar, Gabriel saw that he had successfully taken out the entire backup squad that had arrived on behalf of the Circle. Looking to his right, he saw Alex and Kristen against the far wall, both bleeding. Martin Bishop walked out from behind a pillar only to find Ariel lying on the ground gasping for breath in front of him. The grenade that Gabriel had thrown had collapsed her lung from the concussion. Martin stood over the helpless Ariel for several seconds before raising his weapon.

"Go to hell," gasped Ariel.

Martin didn't respond to Ariel's taunt. He looked deeply into the woman's eyes and pulled the trigger placing a bullet in her forehead.

Martin Bishop seemed to relish his kill, standing over Ariel's body. He looked up to see his daughter walking toward him. The quiet of the expansive room was now more deafening than when the grenade had gone off. Cady smiled at her father and he smiled back. Before she could reach her father, his smile turned into horror as his chest was ripped open by a single gunshot. Turning to look at his attacker, he spotted Jeremiel standing directly behind him. Martin fell to the ground clutching the wound that the young assassin had just caused.

Jeremiel now pointed his weapon at Cady. She realized that it would be impossible to find cover and closing her eyes; she stood still accepting that she would be the next to die. A single shot rang out, making Cady jump, expecting to feel the pain of a bullet in her chest, but quickly she realized that the shot did not strike her. Opening her eyes, she saw Gabriel lying on the floor in front of her, bleeding from the shoulder.

"Gabriel," screamed Cady as she hunched over to help him.

Gabriel lay on the ground staring at Jeremiel with hate. His realized that he made a mistake letting Jeremiel live after rescuing Kristen from the convenience store. Trying not to show his pain, Gabriel lay motionless at the end of Jeremiel's gun. Cady embraced Gabriel from behind desperately hoping that he would be ok.

"You see Gabe, I keep my promises. I told you days ago that the next time we met things would be different."

"You were right Jeremi," responded Gabriel. "I didn't want to have to kill you, but you leave me no choice."

"Ha, that's a laugh," said Jeremiel. "I'm the one holding the gun Gabe; I win."

"No Jeremi, I win," said Gabriel smiling.

Looking at Cady in horror as she drew a gun from the back of Gabriel's waistband, he had no time to reposition his weapon. Cady fired, emptying the clip into Jeremiel striking him in the chest multiple times.

Gabriel saw Jeremiel fall to the floor, covered in blood. Pulling himself toward Jeremiel, he crawled determined to speak to his apprentice one last time. He reached Jeremiel and looked up to assess his wounds.

"I'm sorry Jeremi, these are fatal."

"It's ok," said Jeremiel calmly. "I had it coming."

"You should have listened to me," said Gabriel.

"I was never good at that was I," choked Jeremiel.

"Jeremi, you were a good friend. I didn't want it to go down this way."

"Gabe, do something for me."

"Anything buddy."

"Go get Abbadon and Michael," said Jeremiel.

"You got it," responded Gabriel sliding Jeremi's eyes shut with his fingers.

Gabriel took the empty weapon from Cady and pulling himself up he embraced her in a hug. His plan had not gone completely the way that he wanted but Cady was alive and that is what mattered most to him. Looking around the room, he saw the bodies of nearly two dozen assassins including Uriel, Ariel and his friend Jeremiel. On the far wall Alex was helping Kristen to stand and Cady had now moved to check on her father. Martin Bishop had been shot by Jeremiel and Gabriel wasn't optimistic about his prognosis. Martin proved to be much stronger than Gabriel had thought however and was also picking himself up off the ground. Gabriel walked slowly toward Martin to check his wound. Although shot in the back, he may be able to survive the wound long enough to get Cady out of the building.

Alex and Kristen limped closer to Gabriel as he examined Martin. Turning to check on everyone else, he could see that everyone but Cady had sustained a serious wound. Alex had a gunshot wound in his side that was bleeding badly enough to be a critical injury. Kristen had been hit in the left leg and right arm, and Martin in the back.

"Thank you guys, for everything," said Gabriel.

"No sweat, Alex said cringing from the wound in his side. "We should all do this again sometime."

"Alex, can you get everyone out of here," asked Gabriel.

"Yea, but what about you?"

"I have some unfinished business to attend to," reported Gabriel.

"Gabe, you're hit. You don't stand a chance against Michael," said Alex.

"I only need to last long enough to give you time to get out of the building," said Gabriel with a confident smile.

Alex knew what Gabriel meant but Cady displayed a questioning look as she held her father up.

"What do you mean," she asked.

"No time to explain, Alex, it's time to put an end to the Choir. Get them out of here now."

Alex nodded and positioned himself on the other side of Martin, supporting his weight. Kristen began limping toward the elevator and pushed the down button. Alex and Cady carried Martin toward the elevator and when they reached the large metal doors, Cady turned to find Gabriel but saw no trace of him.

Chapter 43
Revelations

Walking into another dimly lit room of the Choir's headquarters, Gabriel had refilled his clip from the dead assassins lying around him in the last fight. Gabriel was determined to end the reign of the Choir and tonight would be his only chance. He knew that failure would still spell the death of everyone that fought with him this night and he couldn't let that happen.

The expansive room, Gabriel knew was the place where Michael had trained him to be an assassin. He had spent entire year training in this room, waiting for the time where he would be ready to make his first kill. Ironically, this would be the room where he made his last kill as well. Gabriel's shoulder felt like it was on fire, burning with every movement. He walked into the middle of the room and tried to focus his vision into the darkness.

"I know you're in here Michael. Show yourself so we can get this over with," Gabriel said calmly.

"You shot me little brother," called Michael's voice from the darkness.

"Sorry about that," said Gabriel sarcastically.

"You just don't understand little brother; this never had to happen. If you would have just killed the girl, we could have been a family again," rang Michael's voice as he stepped from the shadows.

Gabriel could see that Michael was bleeding from his left leg and lower back. He had hoped that the wounds would slow his brother down enough to survive the battle but he wasn't optimistic.

"You are the one who doesn't understand Michael. I consider it worse to know that you are my brother and that Marcus is our father. A true family wouldn't want this kind of life for each other."

"Be that as it may Gabriel, we are blood."

"Not my blood," yelled Gabriel as he stepped into the circle of light in the center of the room. "Come on Michael, let's do this one like old times," he taunted.

Without a word, Michael drew his weapon and ejected the clip with Gabriel quickly following suit. Dropping their weapons onto the floor, they reached into the darkness where each of them knew a weapons rack stood from their training. Returning their arms into the light with a samurai sword in their hands, Gabriel was the first to unsheathe his weapon. Michael pulled the sword from its scabbard slowly at first, and then almost unseen whipped the scabbard at Gabriel and attacked.

Gabriel struck a blow at Michael from overhead but it was deflected and the sword's made their first clang of battle. He knew that Michael lived for a good showdown so taking advantage of that fact; he tried to deflect his every advance. Gabriel knew that he had to hold out for as long as possible to give the others time to escape the building. Knowing that it was nearly impossible to beat Michael, especially when he was wounded, Gabriel taunted his brother.

"You're getting soft in your old age," laughed Gabriel.

Enraged, Michael struck several more blows that Gabriel deflected with his sword. The flash of light coming from the swords seemed magical in their appearance as it danced across the blades. Gabriel knew that the reason the center light was activated in the middle of the room was to provide distraction, and they certainly did that with the reflections on the swords.

"Come on brother, this is pathetic, attack me," demanded Michael.

"Are you so anxious to die," taunted Gabriel again.

Michael had enough of Gabriel's taunts and began attacking at full force and speed. The light from the ceiling bounced off of the blades with lightning speed as the swords collided faster and faster Each of the two assassins were proficient with a sword. However impractical the use of a sword was, both Gabriel and Michael respected the personal relationships shared in a duel. This instance was certainly no different as the brothers collided again and again, weapon on weapon. Gabriel decided that it was time to strike, and threw all of his momentum into ducking a high slice from Michael's sword. Spinning as the blade traveled over his head, Gabriel turned and swung catching Michael in the abdomen with his blade.

With a scream, Michael backed out of the fight and moved out of reach.

"I see you have been practicing," said Michael.

"Every day," responded Gabriel.

Michael leapt into the fight once more, catching Gabriel by surprise and cutting deeply into his back. Gabriel felt the burn of the sword as it sliced into his muscle but kept his composure, spinning to meet another of Michael's blows. Michael leapt at Gabriel once more this time lowering his sword to slice under Gabriel's catching him in the leg. Gabriel fell to one knee but quickly recovered. Michael was still on top of him, coming faster than before with a jab. Gabriel managed to block the point of Michael's sword with his, but Michael spun his sword back onto his target and struck Gabriel in his right shoulder causing him to drop his sword and fall to the ground.

"It really is a shame brother. I didn't want to have to kill you," said Michael as he moved the tip of his sword to Gabriel's chin. "Everything that you have done up to this point will be undone when I kill you; don't you understand. The girl will still die, along with her father and Alex."

Gabriel felt a renewed vigor flow through him at the mention of harming Cady. He slapped the blade of the sword away with his open hand and quickly recovered his blade stabbing Michael through the heart. Gabriel stood face to face with his brother with fire in his eyes. He didn't care about being killed by Michael, but if killing his brother was the only way out of this for Cady, he was happy to do it. Michael fell to his knees, and then crumpled onto his side lifeless.

Gabriel felt his strength being drained by the amount of blood he had lost during the fight. He knew that his wounds were too severe to continue. Closing his eyes and falling to the floor, darkness surrounded him, but the thought of Cady made death acceptable. He would die knowing that she still loved him. From the shadow's Gabriel could hear her voice. Imagining for a second that he had already died and was in heaven, Cady's voice called his name in the darkness. Gabriel thought of the moments that they had shared in Las Vegas and it warmed his heart to remember the love that they had shared. Drifting off, his last thought was of Cady before everything went black.

Chapter 44
Forever's End

Gabriel awoke minutes later next to his dead brother. Michael lay on the floor with his eyes wide with surprise. Gabriel pulled himself up and limped toward the room where his friends had fought for their lives. Limping over several bodies on his way to the elevator, he found that the large doors were already open, awaiting a passenger. Stepping inside and pressing the button for the lobby, the elevator descended. When the doors opened he found that Alex had gotten everyone out of the building safely. Looking through the large glass doors in the front of the building, he spotted the stolen SUV that they had procured before parting ways in Nevada. The vehicle sat idling, as if waiting for Gabriel to escape the building. His body was weak; as he walked a trail of his blood poured out of the open wounds that Michael had given him. Falling to his knees, he saw Cady leap from the SUV and run for the front doors of the building. Gabriel had no strength left in his body; he rolled onto his side and watched helplessly as Cady flung open the front door of the building and fell to her knees beside him.

"Gabe, get up, we have to get you out of here," she cried.

"I can't," was all that Gabriel could muster.

"Gabe, Alex is coming to help us, just hang on."

"I can't leave," said Gabriel.

"Why not," Cady cried.

"My father is still here. I have to make sure that he can't hurt you anymore," he said weakly.

"I don't care about him Gabe, let him come, just please get up, we have to go."

Alex finally made it to Gabriel's side kneeling down at the head of his fallen partner. He examined the wounds that he had sustained and shook his head no at Cady signifying that he wouldn't make it even if they could get him out of the building.

"Don't tell me that Alex, we have to try," she screamed.

"Alex, do you have the detonator," asked Gabriel weakly.

Alex nodded his head and pulled a small metal device from his pocket. He held the device for a brief second, then without a word, handed it to Gabriel.

"What is that Gabe," Cady asked weakly.

"It's the detonator for the bomb that he told me to rig in the building," said Alex.

"Cady," Gabriel broke in. "You still owe me from our Blackjack bet."

"That's right I do, that means you have to come with us so I can live up to my end of the deal," she said as tears formed in her eyes.

"I've got to ask that favor of you now. Cady, please do this for me."

"Anything Gabe, anything you need."

"I need you to walk away now."

"GABE NO!"

"Cady, you promised me that you would do the one thing that I asked, and I have to ask it now... Please walk away."

"No Gabriel, no please don't do this. You promised me that we could be together forever."

Gabriel slowly raised his up to Cady's face and brushed away the tears that were falling to the floor as they had been the night before.

"Cady, I love you so much," said Gabriel even more weakly than before.

"I love you too Gabe," she said just as weak.

"It's time to go honey; I can't stay awake much longer. Please, go."

"Gabe," said Alex putting his hand on his dying partner.

"Take care of her Alex," said Gabriel.

"You got it," he responded.

Cady refused to leave Gabriel's side, but Alex knew that they needed to evacuate the building. Out of the corner of his eye, he saw the elevator light switch on.

"We've got company Gabe. Are you ok to do this?"

"Yes," he said. "Cady, it's time to go. Please remember that I will always be with you."

"Gabe," was all she could muster before Alex helped her to her feet and began forcing her back out of the building. "Gabe, I love you," Cady screamed as the front doors closed behind her.

As the elevator door opened, Marcus stepped out accompanied by several reinforcements. Gabriel recognized most of the men accompanying Marcus as trainees. The trainees were young men who had been recruited to be assassins; young men, who would never live to make their first kill. As Marcus approached Gabriel's unmoving body, he stared out of the front door only to see the white SUV pulling away. Bending down to Gabriel, Marcus looked enraged.

"You failed son. I will find her," he said.

"I doubt that," responded Gabriel.

"Why so confident Gabriel?"

Gabriel could not bring himself to say another word to his bastard father. Opening his hand, he showed his father the detonator. Marcus's eyes widened with surprise. Standing up and turning to the other assassins Marcus tried to break into a run but it was too late. Gabriel activated the switch with his thumb and in a flash of blinding light, all of his pain, worry, and fear disappeared. All he could feel was love; true, selfless, unbridled love for the girl that he had met only two weeks ago. In that moment, Gabriel knew that he would still be able to watch over Cady. He could still be there to protect her as he always had been. On earth he was the fallen, one who betrayed the Choir to protect that which he loved most in the world, but in spirit, he would always be her guardian angel.

Epilogue
One Year Later

Cady Bishop stood at the gates of the Shaver Lake graveyard. One week after Gabriel sacrificed himself for her, after their wounds were healed, Agent Kristen Shamhat, Martin Bishop and Alex Brody parted ways. Since then she had not seen Alex or Kristen, but the promise that they made together held true in her heart. Everyone agreed that one year after Gabriel's sacrifice; they would meet at his empty grave to see him one last time. Since the installation of his headstone in the small town where he appeared just one year ago and saved her life, she stood awaiting Kristen and Alex. Out of the corner of her eye, she spotted a black SUV, similar to the one that Gabriel had driven pulling onto the winding road leading to the cemetery. Cady's heart jumped into her throat, wondering if her wish had come true, wondering if Gabriel would step out of the vehicle and she could fall into his arms.

In her dreams, she is standing at his grave and Gabriel appears before her asking her to move on, but she always refuses. Since the night that Gabriel died, she has held hope in her heart that he would come to her rescue once again. As the SUV pulled up to the gates of the cemetery, she couldn't make out who was driving the vehicle. Closing her eyes and imagining Gabriel stepping out of the vehicle, she smiled a warm smile. When she opened her eyes, she saw that Alex was stepping from the passenger side of the vehicle. The driver's side door opened and Agent Kristen Shamhat exited. Cady's hopes died with the vision of Kristen walking toward Cady.

"Hi Cady," said Kristen with a warm smile.

"Kristen," she responded as they hugged each other.

Breaking away from Kristen, she reached out to hug Alex, who was standing at her side.

"How're you holding up Cady," asked Alex.

"Little by little," she said weakly. "How about you two"

Kristen pulled herself closer to Alex and took his hand, both of them displaying a wedding band.

"That's great," said Cady with a smile.

"We figured that life was too short to be engaged so we went to Vegas and got hitched last month," said Alex.

"I'm really happy for you two," said Cady.

Without another word, Alex pushed open the gates of the cemetery and the three of them stepped onto the grounds. Only fifty feet from the gate, overlooking Shaver Lake, stood a solitary headstone.

Gabriel Mason
Born: June 15th 1987—Died:
Goodbye our fallen angel

Alex had a confused look on his face as he stared at the headstone. Cady seemed to pick up on his confusion and turned to him with a weak smile.

"Even I didn't know his birthday, how did you find it," asked Alex.

"I didn't know it either, so I put the date that he became a good guy; the day that he saved my life. I couldn't bear to place the date of his death on it. I know it's stupid, but I feel like if I do that, then he is really gone. I want to feel like he is still with me, always."

"That's not stupid," said Kristen. "I know he is out there somewhere watching over you."

Alex turned to see Martin Bishop walking toward the grave with a blanket cradled in his arms. Alex lost his breath as Martin reached the grave.

"Sorry we're late honey, he just didn't want to let me dress him this morning," he said.

Cady reached out and took her son into her arms, cradling the small boy. Alex and Kristen both looked amazed at what was happening. *Cady has a baby*, they thought in unison.

"Sorry I didn't tell you before, but I wanted his first visit to his father's grave to be special."

Alex's mood brightened as he stared into the warm green eyes, which he knew so well.

"Gabriel would be so proud to be a father," said Alex as he let the baby boy squeeze his finger.

"Yea, I wish he could have known him," said Cady with a tear falling from her face. "Do you think he knows about him?"

"Oh I think he knows. Not much gets by him, that's for sure," said Kristen.

"What is the little guy's name," asked Alex, with a hunch that he already knew the answer.

"Gabriel," said Cady proudly. "His name is Gabriel."

After paying their respects, Alex and Kristen walked slowly back to the black SUV that they shared. As they crawled inside, a voice from the back seat asked the question that Alex dreaded to answer.

"How is Cady?"

"She's good Gabe," said Alex trying to hide the fact that he had a son.

"I wish that you could have let her know that you survived the blast," said Kristen.

"If I did that then she would be on the run again. As long as any remaining members of the Choir think that I am dead, she will be safe," said Gabriel.

"I guess you're right," said Kristen sadly.

"You ready," asked Alex.

"One more question Alex."

"Shoot," he said.

"How is my son?"

Alex had hoped that Gabriel didn't know about the boy, but thinking back to what Kristen had said in the cemetery, *not much gets past him.*

"He is beautiful Gabe."